VIKING

[THE JUNGLE TURNED BLACK]

JOHN BOWIE

RED DOG
UK

Published by RED DOG PRESS 2022

First Edition

Paperback ISBN 978-1-914480-14-0
Ebook ISBN 978-1-914480-15-7

www.reddogpress.co.uk

For love, family and art.
Nothing else matters.

'I step out, my internal fire re-stoked, ready to face my demons, fight if need be and win.

I'm raging, focused. Like a jungle warrior after his second bowl of tiger-cock soup.'

— *John Bowie, Untethered*

'I ain't goin' out like the rest. Burned down to a smouldering heap waiting to be put out by tomorrow's rain. Fuck that shit. I'm overdue settling down, putting my feet up. I tell ya, Sinbad. You listening? I've killed enough time... and people. This is my golden ticket. The Fatman is leaving the building. Now, don't fuck it up for me. Or I'll get mad. All we have to do is rob this island full of rich fucks and sail off into the sunset. Or, you can set sail. I'll catch the first big-bastard-luxury yacht and be gone from that steaming hot shit hole you call home. Now, are you bastard pirates for hire or not? Yes?! Then, get-to-fucking-work!'

— *Words of a large sweaty American man on a mobile. Overheard by a homeless local girl in Kowloon Market, Hong Kong, as she hid in crushed card boxes at his feet.*

1

NEW BEGINNINGS

JOHN LOOKED UP and smiled at the back of the plane headrest in front as if it was a window to an unspoilt garden. He never thought it could be this way. But then, he never thought he'd order a Bloody Mary without the vodka. He looked at their rings wrapped together in a vice tight grip as they defied their past and rewrote the future.

Their hopes were carried in their inscriptions:

New Beginnings & Adventure Together

A new start.

They'd seen enough hurt and had worked to make things different. Hard enough? —they didn't know yet; for now allowing themselves some benefit of the doubt. It was their honeymoon after all.

By the time the Virgin Marys with extra Tabasco and pepper hit their plastic fold-out tables, it seemed to them as if she'd never bled for him, and he hadn't killed, and both of them were just pure, innocent, love-drunk souls holding hands, flying east on honeymoon.

It would take more than turbulence they were about to hit to shake them.

They drank their drinks and ordered more. The memories of booze burnt his throat conjoined in hurt with the extra Tabasco. Pleasure and pain never that far apart.

All passengers were oblivious to the rapidly changing weather outside. But it would soon touch them hard and shake their realities.

John and Cherry had been through personal wars and rode the plane to a better place. Although inside him, eating away, there was this nagging seed of doubt. That they'd ever be rid of their past—but, they had to try.

'Ever miss it?' she said looking at his dry drink.

'No,' he lied.

He looked outside to the changing mood as the first of many raindrops hit the window. His stomach turned, knowing the drink, smoke and violence would always be an angry blood-thirsty tiger in the jungle: watching and waiting, thirsty for more.

JANET, AN AIR hostess, 27-years-old, made 40 by the caked-on company make-up, peered around a thick black curtain. She felt the plane struggling with the emotional weight carried in aisle 22—she knew they were unlike the rest of the passengers. Could see it. Feel it.

The couple were carrying more than their fair share.

She'd seen it before too. Could read the signs of buried pain. Janet had a knack for tuning into hidden hurting. Passing strangers and the static of their expressions and postures as they kidded themselves to get by. Everyone had something. Some more than others. Some, breaking under the weight—even if they didn't know it yet. But she could see it. To exist with those nagging seeds of doubt; splinters of pain. She'd seen it up close and as personal as anyone could bear.

When her mother had kept her illness from her—those senses were heightened and after her death, they never subsided, forever left in tune with those dark ebbs and flows that most of us ignore... until it's too late.

Once, there was this really bad one on board. A real stinger of a passenger she'd never forget. Five years ago, on a long-haul flight to New York. A man sat in his seat brooding. She'd dismissed it as long as she could, then kept asking him if he was okay.

Clearly, he wasn't and never would be.

His signs were screaming out. Like a collapsing dam of black water. His mind and body were the walls, crumbling in front of her.

His intensity grew like he was feigning interest in the beautiful skies outside, but he looked as if all he saw was the fires of Hell. The guy drank tea, earl grey with a slice. Played with the napkin and just kept on staring. Fiddling. Fidgeting.

He was more than a nervous flyer. Much more. The *signs* were strong.

It made her nervous too.

His mouth smiled but his eyes didn't.

Janet felt it back then and she felt it now with these two in aisle 22. They weren't fooling anyone, she thought, least of all themselves. They weren't scared though. Damaged yes, she thought—felt—but used to it. On a vacation from hurt; knowing they'd have to return.

Eventually, she saw that jittery fidgeting man from five years ago in the papers. Apparently, he'd gotten off her plane, hired a car, drove to a conference centre and walked straight up the aisle.

The evangelist-fake-healer on stage hadn't got to *that bit* in his act quite yet. The bit when he started pulling pigs guts from gullible audience members and claiming their tumours were gone. All for the price of the ticket and anything else they could spare into the buckets that were passed around before they left.

The papers said the man from the plane didn't wait for the main act, apparently he'd had his own performance ready— demanded his own fix for the pain he carried. He'd lifted up his shirt and pointed to where his own incurable cancerous mass was bulging under his grey taut skin.

They said he hadn't eaten properly in weeks. His stomach contents showed the corner of a plane napkin, a rind of lemon and earl grey tea.

The report said the audience noted the evangelist had looked shocked, nervous, and started playing with his not so hidden earpiece. They all knew it was there. Ignorance is blissful and all that. He'd whispered out the corner of his mouth, not so secretly, as his eyes darted around the room looking for backup.

Anyone. Someone.

Meanwhile, the audience was on the edge of their seats awaiting the new miracle. Was this a new set piece? A sight to behold?

They were going to get one.

The man from the plane was so close he must have noticed the wire in the evangelist's ear and could hear the voice on the other end too: 'This isn't part of the act, Max, abort now. Get out! Get out now! Close it down. We've got another crazy,' Went over the tannoy. In a panic, the control room or evangelist had hit the wrong switch.

The audience started to move.

The papers said a fortnight earlier a middle-aged woman with lymphoma had wrestled him to the floor and kissed him. He was then sick in one of the buckets filled with dollar bills at the side, she was forcibly taken away and his charade continued to the eager audience who saw it as a demonstration of his powers. Vomiting out the woman's tumour.

This was different. His back-up did look like they'd save him.

Speculation in the headlines posed that as far as the man from the plane was concerned this evangelist was his last hope.

One read:

FAITH NO MORE.
FAKE HEALER FAILS TO SAVE HIMSELF.

Unlike the last stage invader, the man's suicide note made it clear: he knew it was all an act. Never wanted to admit it, until he was gone.

That's what Janet had sensed on the plane when she saw him.

It was the look on the man's face that Janet recognised: a dying ostrich with its head in the sand. Blinkered by a last shallow hope in the face of sure death. A skydiver pulling an already ripped cord a foot from the ground—smiling on impact.

In the conference hall, the man had acted fast as the audience fled. They ran from what he'd really come to do. To close down the show in a bloody last call of the final performance.

The evangelist was still spurting fresh blood from his neck when the audience finally finished screaming, the last of them exiting the hall in a crazed panic. Passers-by and eager reporters, first on scene and those already there, could hear everything over the approaching sirens.

As the photographers had squeezed in they caught the cover shot of their careers as the evangelist's eyes looked to the high ceiling of the conference hall. As if begging for his own saviour. Then the man from the plane whispered: 'Eat my pain, fake prophet!'

Janet had read it all in the paper on her return flight. Apparently, the evangelist was still alive later on too when the police burst in and took the man from the plane down. He'd used the evangelist's own fountain pen on this so-called preacher's neck and tongue. The man was kneeling with his knees around the preacher's head and had used the pen to cut his own stomach open. The police interrupted him as he was force-feeding chunks of his diseased flesh, his own tumour, a gift. Forcing it into the man already choking on his own blood, saying: 'eat my pain, fake preacher. Eat it all down, feast, prophet. Feast!' over and over again.

'FEAST.'

The tabloids later described two shots echoing around the hall and the man stopping talking. A third shot and apparently he collapsed as the evangelist gasped for life as the tatters of his tongue sprayed a perfect cross in the air. Another money shot for the paps.

The papers knew how to play the symbolism. The irony. Another headline read:

FINAL CALL FOR FAITH HEALER

The accompanying photo was of an empty stage with a bloody microphone on the floor.

Janet knew the man from the plane was finally at rest. But those that had witnessed never would be again. He'd beaten his disease to a resolution. And she was glad the evangelist never preached again. That he couldn't, not without a tongue.

Yes, Janet just knew when people were burying their hurt. Carrying more baggage than her plane could hold, when they were at breaking point.

She recognised it with these two now in aisle 22. They were heavy laden cargo.

'WHAT IS IT with those two?' the other hostess whispered as they closed the heavy curtain together. 'Didn't think we had Sky Marshalls due with us.'

'Not sure they are. They don't normally sit together anyway. These two are something else.'

'Intense newlyweds waiting for a quickie in the toilet?' she smiled and giggled. A dirty laugh exposing a secret.

'Dressed for funerals, smiling at war,' Janet muttered back and faded the hostesses' filth-ridden smile.

'Gonna be a long haul again.'

'Just hope it's a smooth ride,' Janet sounded nervous as the plane started to shake violently. They were flying into a wall of pitch-black clouds.

The couple in aisle 22 were both smiling in the face of the storm.

Janet wasn't buying it.

WRAPPED IN THE eye of the storm, nature tested their resolve and the strength of the plane with turbulence as cracks of lightning strobed the inside of the cabin. The plane's lights flashed and its metal groaned, and rivets squeaked, as passengers' stomachs were pushed into chests and the pressure drops came again and again.

Crack. Drop. Screams all around. Except in aisle 22.

The passengers nearly all broke down, even the pilot's heart appeared to skip a beat or two as the plane plummeted in the sudden pockets of air. Again, and again, without rest. Without warning.

The dials went haywire and the co-pilot reached for a sick bag. 'I'm sick of this shit. Are we not there yet already?'

'Cool it, Reg', all in the training. Just buckle up and ride it out,' the captain managed to speak, just, then pointed for the co-pilot to pass him one of the bags for himself.

Everyone screamed in the back. Except for that couple dressed all in black—newlywed and unshakeable.

Three children pissed themselves, an old lady at the front held her chest like it was expanding its last breath, as a large American man in aisle 3, who'd paid for only one of the two seats he was using with his huge arse, nearly shat himself. He gripped the armrests as his knuckles turned as white as his face as his knuckles pushed hard at his stretched skin.

There was another sudden drop and the old lady in the front row brought her hands together to pray it was the last. 'Please, god. Not like this. I want to see them one last time.'

The couple in aisle 22 kept smiling on through the chaos, having endured hell, nothing would touch them. But, like the turbulence, with the fading lightning and fear around them— the shock of a fall was always sure to be close by. Ready to release that blood-thirsty tiger that waited patiently to pounce.

2

MICRO HOTEL

THE MICRO-HOTEL room had no windows. Total isolation. A three square metre cell filled with stale air. It had little floor space and vibrated with the air con units on the wall outside. The relentless traffic noises never stopped either, day or night, mixing with the sounds of the busy street market stalls below that buzzed and chattered like a concert interval. The room was tiled everywhere: floor, ceiling, walls and on the furniture so that everything echoed across and bounced off its unsympathetic hard surfaces.

Their breath hung in the air and then slid down the tiles, slowly dripping down. A caged sensuality filled the air. It was like the room had its own version of time too. Or no time at all.

Slowed. Distorted. Disconnected.

They were in this small box of a hotel room by choice and it was as if the outside world didn't exist anymore to them. It secured the feeling in them that no one would ever know where they were.

They could do anything. Uninterrupted.

Time, place and the outside world had become abstracted by what they had become: truly together.

It was perfect.

John, the boy in the bubble, a loner had now become two. Wrapped in love, sealed in that windowless room with the focus solely on each of them. Lives on hold with united hearts on cloud nine.

'I love our little cell,' Cherry said, undressing for the shower as he lay on the bed with his feet up on the tiled wall. Neither of them considered themselves particularly tall but the room made them feel like giants in a doll's house.

'You know how they get reluctant animals to breed in captivity?'

She smirked at his brutish blunt hint at the inevitable sex to come, 'I'm sure you'll tell, or show me...'

'They just put them together in smaller and smaller boxes.'

'Really?' She picked up a towel, looked for somewhere to put it. Saw there was no space and threw it over his head.

He kept talking from under the damp rag. 'Yes... and if still, no magic happens after a few days. Their box gets made even smaller...and smaller. Eventually, it's inevitable. One body part of one animal has to go into the other. There's simply no space left,' he looked out from under the towel. Peaking, cheekily.

'Are you saying you like our little box? This hidey-hole we have here? Or are you saying we're going to do it?'

'It has all we need,' he looked at her. 'Great stop off before KL,' he looked deeper into her. Like she was that bottle of scotch he couldn't have, and as if he still allowed himself a drink.

'Not sure the lack of windows will help with the jetlag,' she bent over.

Everything was about an inch from his face.

His eyes widened further and he stopped himself growling. An involuntary animalistic impulse. Up until recently he'd spent a lifetime in the darkness and had forgotten what beautiful was, let alone the scent. Now here she was in front of him after travelling for twenty hours still looking and smelling beautiful. 'You gonna wave *that* at me all honeymoon I expect?'

'If you're lucky,' she said, arched her back, turned and smiled. And what was left of the world dissolved? Even the hard shell of the room about them had become nothing.

Both of them, and them alone, was all that mattered. Nothing else could.

It was a tiny room with an even smaller shower. They managed to fit together. The sweat dripped from them and the walls when they got out in a rolling sheet. A river of moisture. No distractions.

All that existed…was each other.

KOWLOON MARKET BOOMED, clattered, raced and bustled. Rushing as the people swarmed to manically produce, share, eat and harangue amongst themselves. A deal here, another there and a barter there. The people were like a mass of swarming busy ants as they carried, cooked and hurried to and fro.

Never barging. Never impolite. Perfectly in harmony.

The people were the blood of the market flowing effortlessly about the passageways that were its veins, stall to stall, which were arteries bursting with produce. The pavement and paths were worn and shiny from hundreds of years of this, maybe much longer. Glossy, finished like a fine varnish by the resident food and fish oils spilt and walked into it. Any oilless moisture evaporated up with the steam and smoke of constant activity and that non-stop friction between the bodies driving busy feet across the ground.

Noises and smells about them were as constant as the visuals, all around the scenes changed and moved as if painted as frantically as a Jackson Pollock but as rich as a Da Vinci.

John and Cherry walked through it all, aware, but fairly immune. As if wearing a calming force field that kept the melee at bay. And as if the concrete tiled shell of the Micro Hotel was all around them still.

Their mobiles were switched off and they'd avoided any connection to the Western World. Newspapers, screens and messages were all ignored as they minimised the risk of being dragged out of their contentment at any point by a real-world announcement. A slap in the face by a world they had left behind. The same world that seemed to disown them and had forced their hands to this point.

Occasionally, something would break through their defences. A clue, hint or action. John's hackles would still rise even if his mind was partly distracted by a greater power. The hairs on the back of his neck and his senses would heighten. Focus. And each time he'd calmly fix on the words of their ring inscriptions: 'Adventure Together'. And he'd stroke his wedding ring finger with his thumb of the same hand. Drifting back into that better place it made. Carved out of all that hurt and made good.

He could tell her instincts were still attuned also. He loved her for not drawing attention to it. With time he hoped the battles of yesterday would fade and these warring instincts with it.

They sat eating noodles at a street vendor's make-shift cafe and John jumped a little as the chef clattered his knives down behind him. He could feel the blades. Razor-sharp. Cutting through the neck of the chicken as it withered to be free. Wings flapping, blood dripping as a soaked feather or two dropped in a steaming pool by the chef's feet. Something beautiful and light floating on the most visceral of substance: blood. Black like oil. Still warm as its steam rose to the air.

'Ever considered becoming vegetarian?' she said and smiled across the table at him.

'A little now.'

'Really?'

'One thing at a time though, I think,' he said while taking a drink of tea.

Across the small market stall, three trellis tables behind Cherry a large American man started to shout on his mobile. Not enough for John to hear clearly but enough to distract from the harmonious noise and clatter of Hong Kong's street market that they'd come to hide away in.

'Never that far away from one,' Cherry said. 'Australians and Americans.'

'And rats,' he said.

'It's the same back home.'

'It's what they often say about the Chinese,' he started to stroke his ring finger with his thumb.

Calm. Stilling. In love.

The large American continued his mobile phone tirade and John could see a little girl cowering in boxes near his feet. The big man lifted a tabloid newspaper off the table with the other hand. Flapped it angrily around like the bird that had just been gutted.

John caught a flash of an incomplete headline from the newspaper.

Keywords. Nothing more:

EX-IRA, LADS TO BE RELEASED.
BOMBS AWAY.
JUSTICE IS DEAD.

John looked to the tabletop, took a sip of tea, then stroked his ring finger harder this time. Feeling the pressure down to the bone of his finger. The return to serenity was temporarily broken. But it wouldn't last.

'Careful, you'll wear a hole in that.'

'I love you,' John mouthed. Forcing his emotions back on track and away from the newspaper he'd only half-glimpsed. Ghosts from his past. They were always there to be found— their secret would be to stop looking. These ghosts, it would seem, were to be given freedom. Just as he thought he'd found his own.

In the background, the large American slammed the tabletop again and again. Bang. Bang. As if he was placing an angry bet. His nostrils flared and blotched red-faced.

Negotiating.

Ordering someone.

Touring Americans all looked the same to John. Over assertive. Self-medicated and emotionally overly self-assured. Made superior through generations of training, therapy and brainwashing.

John felt it: takes one to know one.

'I. Love. You,' John mouthed across to Cherry.

'Ele-phant-juice-too,' she mouthed back.

They both giggled, stood and walked back into the melee of the market. High on each other and for now bulletproof again.

They reclaimed their moments together as the image of the big American temporarily faded.

3

HMP MAZE

THE LADS, JAKE and Pete, had gone inside as boys, barely eighteen; keen foot soldiers following orders at the time. 'Yes' men. Or, just blood-thirsty boys eager to move up the ranks.

Savage minds. Feral dogs.

Imprisoned for a crime they almost committed… as their release date neared, they'd soon grown into men, firmly giving orders out: barks and whispers all taken as gospel with a threat of violence regularly followed through on. Some deserved, some, to feed the hellish nature in them.

As their mothers had always said: they had the Devil inside. And he liked it in there with them as much as they did. Fed him all he needed.

They'd carved out a powerful show for themselves in HMP Maze. Knives and bombs stabbing out from behind their eyes— no one fucked with that. Everyone knew what they were capable of on the outside to those that didn't deserve it. And on the inside, to those that did.

They ruled the prison corridors. Some more than others. Building up an elite inner circle by evolution and cruel design. They'd had time to work at it; set a standard. Bitter harmony in motion. Fellow inmates were puppets and the wardens were irrelevant specs of shit. To be scraped off at every opportunity. Another uniformed authority damned to hell. Like those outside that had damned them to be inside. The guards were mere flies to them, creeping around the concrete shell and exercise yard. Powerless.

The lads had a new world order and blood fixed on those savage minds. Both raging bulls with hatred for the world.

The authorities would have done well to keep them and their comrades firmly behind bars. But the red tape faded and frayed... and the boys had been working hard on perceptions to fix outcomes in their favour. They'd had plenty of time for that too; rabid dogs behind a curtain of deceit, with an altar boy image on show for all those key stages: the review panels. And best behaviour in corridors as they padded meekly about them, acting submissive—good lads. Reformed and remade.

IRA allegiance was fixed but buried firmly behind them. No ties to worry about. Both sides knew they were better off unassociated in order to carry out their business going forward. The lads had the approval to go rogue. Free-range evil without a cause or flag to taint by their behaviour. Previously sanctioned or otherwise.

They'd found their calling in a nihilist group that grew up around them; bad seeds feeding off hatred and spilt blood. All these were made up of ex-terrorists, hardened criminals and ex-neo-nazis. Most had left their ideologies behind them and followed the lads' general resentment of 'the system' and any imposed authority. They attacked and berated the world, system and the crony politicians too, they were damned most of all. They had backed it all up as far as the lad and their crew were concerned.

The bad seeds all grew interwoven together. In the end, Jake and Pete grew to be the roots of the trees that sheltered and trained them all.

They all hated control—looked to break it.

Most people asked for it, a bashing and most systems needed it, a reset. So, they'd decided: these times they lived in, demanded it. And they were the cure to everyone's malaise and discomfort. They looked to break everything, reveal pure pain and from this people would be forced to re-evaluate their shitty existences.

That's what they preached.

Soon, to be practised.

Often, the criminal over-philosophising waned and the lads just wanted everywhere to be the Wild West. Just with more guns and whores. Both bigger, slacker and easier to come by. They lived in their heads, backed up by the Devil, and it was an evil depraved place to be with no redemption, so they chose to damn everyone to hell with them. Dragging them to a blood bath.

The prison priest had worked hard to convince them of their irreversible sins. That they couldn't undo anything, but could only go forward minimising the hell-fire to come. They knew they'd burn. So, they followed their instincts—and it was that of a wild bloodthirsty pack of dogs.

The group they'd formed didn't have a name for a long time, then a song came on the radio, they liked a disconnection and ill-feeling in the lyrics and went with that: *The Untethered.*

It didn't last. Too obscure. Raised too many questions when they had work to do.

Then, the next name, the name *Transference*, which lasted about a week. Then, *The Division.* All taken from an author's books they'd found the prison's tired dog-eared library.

The author's first book was *Untethered*, maybe he'd liked the song too? — they'd thought.

They had this connection to the author. Bound in blood. He could have shot them, didn't, and so ruined their martyrdom.

He'd refused to shoot them in Ireland. He was S.A.S. or Special Forces at the time, not an author at the time. He'd been disgraced and discharged from service for not killing them, and they liked that. The savage lads. Through his inaction, he'd become an unwanted, burning black sheep—just like them.

Everyone was disgraced, and they were both still alive. So was he. Wishing he wasn't. It meant the lads got locked up rather than buried. Destiny, it would seem, had woven them all together with this now writer-fella, so they felt a bond. An unsaid thanks in their Shakespearian tragedy.

So, they looked to his books to complete the circle. Fate, a clenched fist squeezing all their angry bodies together until bones started to break and the blood vessels burst in their eyes.

The Devil's symphony in each breath they took inside and in the words *he* typed outside.

Eventually, they stopped thinking of names for their gang, got back to work. Scheming, and planning more deaths. When they got out and the work was done, maybe, they'd look the author up. Look him straight in the eyes, and ask him: after all that they'd done since if he wished he'd taken those shots back then.

Taken them out. Stopped the killing.

And if he had done, where would he be now? Would he have anything to write about? If history was unwritten... would he be playing happy families on a beach somewhere? With a wife maybe? A family? Or, would his bloodthirsty draw, as the power of the sun, be as just as inevitable as their own fates. Burning. A searing heat. Regardless of if their paths had all crossed or not.

Moral restraints and judgements riled them as much as money and structure. In their worlds, it was deserved that this author, ex-SAS footsoldier, had ended up in his own literary Hell by trying to do the right thing. Who was he to decide right and wrong? Jake and Pete's right and wrong came by seeing the world bleed. How was this author so different?

He wasn't.

He'd soon see. When he realised the bomb was always going to go off. All he did was delay the fuse. Grow its burn.

Because John didn't shoot, the lads were caught alive and locked up for planning an attack on the mainland. When they eventually got out, they'd planned to pick up where they left off and turn the hurt-dial up so that John Black, if that was his real name, heard about it.

Wherever he was hiding he'd feel the vibrations.

Their bombs would shake the world. Make it bleed like a river.

Being on best behaviour in the prison classes, yard and mess hall meant that this release was assured. Planning behind closed doors and in the showers gave them a new purpose for when they did get out.

The bomb.

They were on a treadmill. It wouldn't stop until Hell broke loose.

The visitor had made sure of it.

SLAP. JAKE'S HAND went down hard on the plastic table in his cell.

Pete looked down. Pensive. A ticking bomb.

The scribbled map and notes on the sheet of paper had been scrawled over hundreds of times. Childish illustrations, showing bodies ripped apart, limbs flying, geysers of blood were accompanied by black hate-filled words in harsh capital letters:

FUCK. THEM. ALL.

'This is it,' Jake said. Not long now, brother.'

'Aye, it is. Not long at all, Jakey,' Pete agreed.

'What we set out to do all those moons ago. It's on. This time we'll finish the job. It's for us… no one else,' Jake didn't blink.

The door to the cell opened a fraction. Creaked. A pointed face with spectacles peered around. A weasel and a wimp. He was already in deep, out of his tightly wrapped comfort zone. Totally out of context. All the inmates knew it. He should have been in a softer ward, an open prison maybe. But, times were tight, resources were low. So sheep like him were thrown in with the wolves. No chance.

Jake grabbed the paper and scrunched it up and looked at the door. 'What the fuck do you want?'

'To come back into my room… maybe?' his eyes showed regret instantly at the use of 'maybe', but it was too late to take back. His fate was sealed. Maybe that's what he wanted all along? He winced and looked over his shoulder as if considering a retreat back out into the prison jungle.

'Whilst he's in here, it's ours. Not fuckin' yours. Understand, suit-boy?' Jake pointed a well-gnawed finger at Pete— his brother in arms—then at the face peering around the door.

'Have you two not finished… conspiring?' the weaselly man whispered with another mistaken use of a word. He whimpered a little at the error. As if that made it less cocky to them.

Jake tensed.

Pete slowly stood and beckoned the newly arrived, convicted money swindling businessman into the cell. And in he came, a lamb to the slaughter, and one of them closed the cell door behind him with a clunk of heavy metal.

The businessman had made a mistake or two that would scar him into the afterlife.

They'd make sure of it.

'What do you know about conspiring, friend?' Jake was cold, didn't look up. His words weighed down, threatening what was to come.

Pete laid his back against the door, stronger than any lock, and took a toothpick out of his pocket and casually chewed the end. Looking about the room like he was casually waiting for an imagined dog to take a shit he wouldn't pick up.

There was nowhere for the businessman to go now. Only pain waited.

'I just wanted a rest, to lay down a while. Pete's going in a sec, isn't he? Just thought you'd finished your secret chat. I haven't slept in days.'

'No secrets here, friend.'

Another clumsy word dropped.

Pete slowly walked behind the shamed businessman, grabbed him by the shoulders and forced him down on the chair. Jake stood up from his, just enough to take the toothpick from Pete's mouth and then sat back down again slowly. Menacingly.

'Someone's either heard… or seen… too much here. Haven't they, friend? Haven't they just?' he growled through gritted teeth on the repeat. 'Maybe a little too much of both.' Jake pointed the toothpick at each of the businessman's eyes. One at a time. like he was taking aim or picking one to pluck.

The shell of the room echoed with hate.

No escape.

'No, Jake, no… I'm sorry. I was just wanting a rest is all. Please? Come on, I'll fix you up on the outside. Wash your money. Make you some. You won't have to work again. It's all

I know how. I'll make it up to you. I'm sorry, Pete. Jake. I really am. PLEASE.'

Money meant little to Jake and Pete. They took what they wanted. Always had.

'What do we want with your filthy money?' Pete said.

'You didn't read the brochure did you boyo? Before taking this trip...' Jake continued. 'This isn't a holiday camp. Or, some fucking luxury dingy or whatever the fuck you lawyer types fuck around on when ain't stealing of the common folks.'

'I'm just a business owner... not a lawyer.'

'You say potato...' Jake started.

'I say fucking spud...' Pete finished.

'And I say you're full of shit, little man,' Jake went on.

Outside the cell, the lads were on best behaviour and on track to an early release date. Inside the cell, they were cultivating free-flowing spite against the world... and this businessman, by poking his head around the door, had stuck his head in a hungry lion's mouth. And, when he spoke—he'd hit it on the arse with a stick.

Suicide.

They smelt everything they hated on him. The system and everything they loathed about it. Like blood in the water to a shark. They saw him as much as a criminal as those in Number 10 and Parliament. The prick got caught is all. Was weak at his own game. His corporate kahunas weren't big or connected enough to get him off. He was vermin and crawling lice to the lads. A societal cog in a dog machine they looked to destroy; wrench its legs off and shove them up its arse.

A pair of well-used socks were rammed in the businessman's mouth. They'd been worn and wanked into for months by both lads. He struggled, gagged, wriggled and then his hands were gripped behind the chair. maybe he'd have been sick through the crusty stinking socks if the fear and adrenaline wasn't dominating. His temples visibly pulsed.

Pete forced the man's head to one side and down onto the tabletop.

Jake stuck the toothpick in the businessman's ear as far it would go.

Then an eye. Not too far—just enough.

'Heard and seen too much is all,' Pete said as the man stifled screams, whimpered and cried when they let his head back up.

He spat the sock. Cried.

'Do we have to worry you're gonna talk too much too?' Jake picked up some nail scissors from the sink that had been smuggled in an outside connection's arsehole. Jake stuck his own tongue out and opened the blades around it.

He cut a little. Making himself bleed.

His disregard for his own flesh made the businessman squirm even more. Seeing Jake do this willingly, even enjoy it, to his own body.

The businessman was less than dog shit to them.

JAKE HAD MADE his point. Pete too. They were like the Irish Krays in HMP Maze.

The man cowered in a corner; nowhere to go. Curled into a tight ball. A hedgehog with its spines pulled out. Unsafe from everyone.

He'd just wanted a rest, to lie down.

Now he wanted to sleep forever, and those washed notes and insolvent company trades he'd made were a lifetime away now. They weren't worth it. What was he thinking? He wasn't a real criminal— not like these. And now his eye bled—would he see out of it again? And his ear rang with the pain of a wooden pick rammed into it—would the ringing ever stop?

He wished he'd landed himself in another prison. How'd he get banged up with all these fucking evil terrorists and Neo-Nazis, who knows?

Turned out the pain in his ear canal lasted weeks, maybe a month or so. The lack of hearing and the bloody eye; six months.

The trauma and night sweats never left him.

Outside, he tried to hide but didn't get far. After he was released, they soon caught back up with him. Chained him up like an animal in a piss-filled yard, kept him dependent, and then, when all was lost, they set him to work. They'd finished what they'd started on his right eye and ear. Trophies and reminders to forget everything he'd seen and heard.

He didn't need them for washing notes. He didn't need to talk either.

Turns out they needed a little cash after all. To pay their visitor: the Fatman.

It would seem he wanted cash even if the lads didn't.

4

PULAU TIGA:
PIRATE TRAINING ISLAND

THE IDYLLIC MALAYSIAN island of Pulau Tiga was two and a half hours from Kota Kinabalu by road then another hour by boat. That was it, all it took for Andy and Mark to drop off the map, lose touch with home, board the ferry and enter the heart of darkness in Borneo. Out of sight, out of minds—burying their responsibilities back home.

They had perfect lives on paper: 2.4 children, a BMW and an Audi between them, houses with drives in the suburbs, tired tolerant wives and a textbook work-life balance with enviable golf club memberships. Still, they wanted something more. Had a primal itch to scratch. The affairs hadn't cut it. They looked to break it all down, their packaged up idyllic lives, if only for a week or two. A short time, before returning to their lives in a box. And the damn sorry rat race.

Pulau Tiga island had been used for a reality tv survival programme decades before the band of local pirates took over. Now, giant monitor lizards, troops of feral monkeys ruled the trees and overgrown walkways as fierce fish filled the perfectly azure waters if you went past the shallows. The old film crew's quarters and tv film sets had been reclaimed by the jungle and the pirates who now used it as their base and training camp. A once broadcast haven for Western entertainment, now it was a breeding ground for high seas criminals.

Once this fake paradise was for entertainment, now the island drew locals looking for hard cash for their starving families and people came from even further afield than the starving villages. Much further on a map, a life away culturally— Like Andy and Mark. Some Western hopeful recruits were filled with romantic notions of a wild free life roaming the seas in search of treasure hordes and women. Maybe a bit of rape and pillaging. Others, like Mark and Andy, were more realistic, blood-thirsty and savages. Looking for a personal release without repercussions. Footy hooliganism wasn't enough at home and had lost their draw. Underground fight clubs were filled with people playing at it, pulling punches. They didn't fill the hole either. Filled with suits playing monsters. Actors with no real conviction.

They'd done hours of research, asked around. This isolated island pirate camp was the best they'd found on the dark web. Or, so they hoped.

Locals joined the group for free out of desperation, a last resort to put food on the table, maybe send the kids to get some schooling. Pull their daughters out of the arms of paying sex tourists. They were more aware of the risks. It was the last chance and they knew there was no going back. Westerners, however, like Andy and Mark; they'd paid handsomely. To them, it was a high-end escape. A war game. Until it all came to an end when they'd wash off the blood and board a plane back home to their comfortable lives. So they thought when they bought their tickets. That was the story they told themselves.

The locals couldn't afford that luxury—resented the outsiders, but welcomed their cash.

The fact was: war didn't work like that and pirates didn't bow down to expectations.

The privileged rich clad Westerners, with lives unlived and no suffering, made the pirates and locals sick. Sneering at their scarless clean skins with shallow eyes that had come searching for blood.

Soon, they'd all get it.

MARK AND ANDY had arrived: Pulau Tiga, Pirate Training Camp. They sat on a hot heavenly beach desiring to burn their lives to hell, waiting patiently for their turn to join in the recruitment trials happening behind them in the jungle.

The island was a rich beauty soaked panorama in every direction. There were blue open waters, palm trees and beaches in all directions baking under serene clear skies.

They could hear the shouts, yells and occasional gunshots from the training happening behind them in the jungle. Each snap and bang excited them further as the anticipation rose in both of them—finally there. Free.

Their trials would soon begin. They didn't know what was in store. The deal didn't come with an itinerary, tour guide or glossy brochure.

Both had travelled separately. Strangers at first but came together on the ferry they'd paid for in cash. They both recognised the same look in their eyes: to escape. Living the same lives. Wanting to disappear. And glistening there in both irises of the men there was something much worse. There wrestled an angry tiger, roaring to be set free—a little flash of something horror-filled: to destroy.

Their desire and actions were more common than they'd like to admit. As would be their fate. The island was littered with unmarked graves. Some were left open to the elements as bodies raced to decompose before eager animals, bugs and maggots set in. The animals had developed a taste for human flesh. Supply and demand. Fresh or rotten.

'I can't believe I've finally made it,' Andy looked towards the sun and squinted as a bird flew across the sky, freezing an iconic t-shirt image they might have bought on holiday to touch a sense of escape. Now they were really there.

'Same,' Mark said, 'Such a burnt orange. Almost unreal.'

'When the palm forest fires aren't blotting it out.'

Mark squinted at the sun and held a hand up.

'You left much behind?' Andy asked, with a knowing look. He glanced down at the white band on Mark's ring finger where his responsibilities once shone, emblazoned to tell the world he had made it, was dependable; a real man. Now, the ring was hidden away, like Andy's own, and life. As if he looked to be reborn a delinquent and start over again. If only for a short bloody break.

'You know I have. Same as you I expect,' he looked over to Andy's hand. 'Also, expect you've come to do the same as me too. No? A bit of blood-letting. I'm sure.'

'To kill. Or be killed. Before you do something more regrettable back home? Purge some banality...' Andy conceded and grinned. Not a happy grin. More of someone about to pull their own tooth, knowing the pain was to follow at the slam of a door with string back to an abscessed molar.

Feigned happiness gripped the corners of both their mouths. Sure of the actions they were about to take by their own hands. To regain control. Lost: in a marriage with children. Found: on a beach far away from it all.

Andy grinned even harder. It was an evil thing.

Even those heavenly waters couldn't appease their downward spiralling fate.

They sat together on the beach as cobalt waters lapped, with a perfect horizon that disappeared into straight infinity. A tranquil blanket to a horror building in them, the jungle and the island. It was like floating on a dream as the responsibilities of real lives dissolved into the wet sand at their feet. A dream waiting to be shattered into oblivion. The waters to become blood.

'Look, living dinosaurs everywhere,' Mark gestured at a massive lizard walking towards them down the shore, about seventy feet away.

'Looks big from here. Imagine it up close. Fuck.'

'Hell yeah. Look at that tongue, flicking,' Mark said, gesturing with his own.

The lizard advanced. Rotten or fresh—it would feast.

'What do they eat?' Andy asked.

'What don't they fucking eat? Us, if it gets half a chance. Maybe that's it...' Mark said.

'What?' Andy muttered looking at the huge beast staggering towards them still.

Mark stared at the beast too. 'Our first trial? To face up to this big bastard lizard?'

They both laughed, a little, then looked back at their feet. The big monitor lizard kept walking.

'You know, that tv series based here painted some kind of picturesque and pretty place,' Andy said.

'Is it not?'

'Maybe once. And yes, on the surface it is. Kind of. But dig a little deeper and look at what's actually here. Especially now. Like this big scaly fucker here marching right at us. It's what's here in the honesty of our true eyes without the media filter of tv distorting everything.'

'I think... I get what you mean,' Mark nodded, 'A little,' he squinted as if trying to squash the pretension in the air with his mind.

'Look what's here: the pirates, feral monkeys... that big bastard lizard!' Andy looked at the creature, now about fifty feet away. Getting closer with each staggered motion.

The lizard kept moving towards them. Legs out, slow and jerky but definitely looking fixed on them both in its line of sight.

'Would it try... and eat us, do you think?' Mark said, relaxed and laid himself down then propped up on his elbow to admire the advancing beast.

Thump. Thump.

Both men looked overconfident as if a sheet of armoured glass separated them from its attack.

It was like they were in a dream and not really there at all. The lizard an illusion and them painted or written onto the sands. Their images soon to be washed away. Resetting. Preparing a new canvas for the next pair to try the island.

Andy folded his legs and turned to face the lizard too, fascinated. The giant reptile represented so much they hadn't spoken about. Giving everything up in a reckless disregard for their commitments to others. Running away to play pirates for a few weeks. This was it: the ferocity and that primal calling, up close and personal.

Would they ever go back? Would they get the chance?

The lizard's speed hadn't changed. Slow but determined. Now, thirty or forty feet away. Thump. Thump. It continued and both men glanced at the sand as if feeling the vibrations from the weight of its body on the beach.

'It'd make a good luggage set,' Andy said.

'Good one, Andy. A wallet and a belt for me too. Nice.'

They looked behind at the sound of some new sounds, as barking orders snapped from the tree line. Nothing either of them understood. All foreign.

'That shit directed at us? Didn't hear any of that when it was on tv.'

'Survivor Island was a pussy fest from memory.'

'Fuck knows who that is barking on… When they do want us they know where to find us,' Mark's arrogance was misplaced.

The island was about to take them.

Distracted by the noises behind, the lizard was about ten feet away when they turned back to face it. Their hearts stopped. Suddenly the shit had gotten real. They could smell its rancid breath filled with the decay of its last meal. Razor teeth snapped as a tongue flicked manically. It wouldn't accept a pay-off, small talk or a distraction. Its eyes were clear—it only saw their flesh, meat and bones to crunch. They were food.

In the lizard's eyes, the pair were the next meal.

THE LIZARD LUNGED as both men shut their eyes tight.

'Pussies,' a voice came from behind them.

They weren't the men they thought they were. Only ever used to seeing nature and beasts on tv. They'd disregarded the lack of screen separating them from the heaving lump of nature with teeth that looked to eat them. Normally they'd be sheltered behind a giant flat-screen screwed to the wall—this was upfront, rancid and brutal.

Then came the sound of a thump. And another. A crack of bone.

Andy was first, opened one eye then the next.

Then Mark.

The lizard lay bleeding, two feet away from them. A crossbow bolt in its chest at exactly the right point to stop it and its heart instantly. The shooter stood behind the men and dropped a huge bowie knife and as its blade half pierced into the sand in front of them.

The sun shone through the knife, casting a perfect shadow of the shape of a cross over the men's legs.

'You both. White pussies,' the man barked and laughed.

Andy and Mark were in shock, cowering.

'Skin and gut this thing. Now,' a voice commanded this time from the man.

'What?' Mark and Andy stuttered in unison.

'Yes, you two. Now…If you survive training, you'll be hungry.

They both looked confused.

'This is your food. All you deserve. Shitty lizard guts. Scales,' the man laughed.

'Fuck,' Andy said.

'Shit it,' Mark said.

'Fookin' pussies,' the pirate said and kicked hot sand down their backs. 'Move, cut lizard, now,' clearly he was loving putting the Westerners in their place. Setting the scene for their positions in the pecking order. And in the ecosystem of the island.

Work and obey or die and be eaten.

The training hadn't started and they had landed themselves right in it. Well over their heads.

As Andy went for the knife he glanced at Mark. A look they both shared, there in their eyes. Changed from bloodthirsty to: Where are the skull and crossbones? Bottles of rum? Jolly larking sailors dicking around and killing a few no namers to cross the experience off? Then, back to camp to fuck a wench or two?

This wasn't what they'd signed up to. Taxidermy.

'Wait… survive training?' Mark said, as his and Andy's eyes widened.

They looked around. The Malaysian native, all in black with a crossbow and an AK47, wasn't smiling now.

This wasn't on tv, it was really happening. They'd jumped headfirst into their flatscreens, weren't sure of the plot and had lost control of the remote. They couldn't change the channel.

ARHAA'S NAME MEANT calm, or serene. Increasingly ironic, given how his life was to be turning out. He'd been nothing but bottled rage and fury since joining the pirates. He'd lasted training, gained a few kills and worked his way through the ranks. Now here he stood alongside the training board as recruits ran at it. It was a messy job. But also the most powerful. With hands on who lived and who died— before they'd even started work with them.

The training board was a tattered old sheet of plywood with broken glass stuck to it. A test of courage, self-sacrifice and loyalty. Arhaa knew, despite all this. The birds and reptiles would pick it clean. The chipboard substrate now permanently discoloured from the blood, flesh and guts that had been painted over it in layers of recruits that had failed the ultimate test.

Arhaa's family were a distant echo in his head. Love buried. How could she have known, his mother, that it would come to this? When she picked his name all those years ago? He was a warm new lump pushed into the world. Full of potential.

Arhaa: calm, serene. A joke lost on the sea breeze.

When he was just that little wet lump in a muslin crying on the floor it might have seemed the right thing. A hope to bestow upon him with that name. Whilst in her sorry heart, she must have known then that they'd struggle. Be hungry. Need to adapt.

He evolved.

Arhaa was surprised he'd survived long enough to join the pirates at all. Even more surprised that he lasted long enough to send the increasingly larger bundles of dollars back home. But he was glad he did. Although it was now a home he could never return to. There was blood on his conscience and a furious tiger unleashed. It was what was needed for him to succeed and survive.

Joining the pirates was his last chance to repay her. To pay back his mother for birthing him...keeping him and his sister alive. Now, it was his turn.

Arhaa stood proud and stern alongside the sheet of wood that had been fixed to posts that were deep in the jungle clearing floor. The pirates had chosen this spot out of sight. Away from the landing zones and jetty's that new naive recruits arrived at. The pirate veterans didn't want to spook them too soon.

Now the line of fresh worried faces of new recruits stood in a line. All locals. Now Westerners today, not yet...

Apparently, a couple of new ones had arrived on the Southside beach and Arhaa couldn't wait for their turn to come at his board.

The line of recruits tried to bury their fears, some succeeding more than others. Westerners were a varied bunch. Some were made for this, and had already given up on their lives fully. A delayed suicide of sorts. To others, it was just a game and the board with fixed broken glass on it would be the test that finished them.

Arhaa despised both types. Different in ways he didn't care and similar in that they had more money as individuals than every one of the local recruits put together. Until they took from them.

The splinters of cracked glass glistened in the sun on the board. Bits of material, skin and blood hung, dripped and clung to the board from past trials where the beasts hadn't quite picked it away.

Arhaa felt it was poetry in motion as their legs would carry them at the bloody altar.

Fellow pirates stood on both sides of a straight path, forming a runway from the line of recruits to the upright board. One by one the pirate nearest the line of recruits pointed his AK47 at them and told them when it was their turn to run at the board. Without stopping.

Die by your own hands, fearless, or be shot. If they displayed true commitment they were saved.

It was Arhaa's job to look at the running recruit. Look deep into their eyes as they neared the board, the glass, the impending pain and disfigurement or death by running into it. He knew what he was looking for. In some, it was a determination. Having conceded their fate. The look of someone running headlong into hell and having given up on emotions; fears and hate no longer existing. Some were already devoted. Others showed a transition, usually reshaping halfway down the running strip. Sometimes a few steps away from the board. And Arhaa would pull them to one side. Saving them from the impact of board, broken glass, flesh and bone.

Arhaa was a pirate god. With his hands controlling life and death.

For those waiting in the queue, it was clearly beyond terrifying. Some would see this trial and turn, run and be shot.

Some would simply soil themselves and sob their way up the strip rather than run… and then would be shot. Others would run at the broken glass on the board. Unsure of why Arhaa pulled some aside at the last minute and not the others. Hoping, it wouldn't be them. Risking everything.

Arhaa breathed in deep. Pausing before gesturing.

It was nearly time for another one to run at the board.

He filled his lungs and looked to the sky. He owned it.

It had been clear for so long now the winds always changed and the clear skies would be blackened as the currents pushed the smoke from the palm fires their way and they all stood in a giant cancerous smoking lung.

They were all done for. One way or another.

Arhaa thought of his mother, his sister. How he'd transformed. Hoped he would never meet them again. For their sake. So they wouldn't have to see what he'd become: a monster. If they saw him now they'd be horrified. Ashamed. For only, he knew he had to do it. For them to live. Eat. Breathe.

Time's up. Arhaa yelled for the next one to start running and he could see them trembling on the start line as his comrades smoked, nudged each other with unsaid bets over the fate of the sorry soul about to run.

It happened sooner than usual—the change.

He could see this one's determination as they set off. The fear became something else. Harder. Arhaa recognised it from when he did his own trial. He too turned early. Consigned to a destiny of blood to pay off a debt to his loved ones.

He hated the image of himself. Saved the boy.

Arhaa let the boy, barely a man, run face first into the glass. His body twitched and stopped as he bled out. Another pirate walked over and pulled the body to one side to join a heap of others.

Yes, Arhaa recognised an alternate reality in the boy as he took a final breath. He saved him from that monster he would surely become. Like him.

The jungle parted behind the wide-eyed queue of recruits as two white faces were led at gunpoint through to the back of the queue. They looked, peering around at the board, the bodies. The terrified locals seemed to firm up at the sight of the feeble Westerners, somehow their weakness giving them resolve to prove themselves different from them.

The Westerners looked on, wide-eyed.

Arhaa gestured for the white faces to jump the queue, go simultaneously, next. He would only be able to pull one aside. If he decided to.

The white faces were pushed up the queue at gunpoint. Barrels jabbed into their backs. With unsupportive whispers and mutterings from the others.

From the bushes eyes watched. Animals eager to clean up.

One of the Westerners wet themselves but didn't seem to care. Then they both braced up. As if a steel rod had been rammed down their spines. Possessed. They stood straight with pitch-black eyes.

Arhaa hadn't seen this before; the transformation so soon.

So be it.

Some came to the island to become monsters. Others brought them with them.

5

CONNIE AND TED

CONNIE COULDN'T WAIT to return to the Bullring Shopping Centre. Birmingham City Council had been regenerating it for what felt like ages to her. A lifetime of missed aisle meanderings and empty shopping baskets. She wasn't the only one excited about its reopening. There was sure to be a mad rush and a scramble when Peter Andre cut that red ribbon and the flood gates opened and the place filled and heaved with eager shoppers.

Connie would be there; rain or shine.

The shoppers had all been waiting so long. Precious moments were lost in the delayed construction works. They could have been doing something much more important. They could have been shopping for tat, as her husband Ted would often say.

It was her church. A beacon of distraction from life's frictions and worries.

She'd been saving those little giro cheques, stashing them like a squirrel with its nuts in Winter, desperately wanting to get a little treat for herself and that little something special for that worse half, Ted.

It had been tough for them recently. What with his nervousness at a lump here and blemish there—and not going to the doctors to get checked out. The silly old fool. And then there were the worries at her getting checked herself, knowing her own truths and keeping them from him.

Time wasn't on either of their sides. Not anymore. If it ever was.

The loyal old fool had been through it all. By her side. And her by his.

As they'd both gotten older, things didn't look like getting any rosier. Only hardship, the fragility of old age and whatever came next. But they'd continue to get through it, together. One wobbly step, increasingly more teetering, each day at a time.

Life had been harder still ever since Ted's daughter, from his first marriage, had moved out of the area. That fella she'd met didn't seem to care that Connie and Ted were getting to that stage in life when they needed a little extra help and some support nearby. That they might not be a hundred per cent. For Connie and Ted just to know someone was there on the bitter nights and seasons. At the end of a phone line and close enough to pop by *if* needed.

When…needed.

Ted's daughter's new fella was a career-man. A cheap suit labourer, Ted called him. And, a parasite salesman. This salesman had insisted that he and Ted's daughter move further away, somewhere that suited his dick swinging job and huge big head. Somewhere with a drive to park and show off his big ugly silver BMW: a spaceship to Connie and Ted. It looked like it could eat their little Renault Clio up and crap out the bolts: another thing Ted used to say. Yes, Ted's daughter's man had made it clear he wanted to be somewhere that had a golf course with a fancy nineteenth hole. With nubile waitresses serving behind the bar. Fuelling an inbred soup of bad morals stewing in self-serving Conservative capitalists—this was something Connie would think, but not say. She didn't want to undermine

Ted's sense of intelligence. Unless Countdown was on, or they were playing cards, then she let him have it. Both barrels: boom.

Connie and Ted hated the salesman that stole his daughter away.

The man had driven a stake through their hearts and pushed Ted's daughter further away each day. Why couldn't she have met a nicer man... Not too perfect, no one is. Someone more like Ted. Or, Bobby from the bowls club—another one Connie thought but never said. Ted's ego couldn't handle it and she loved him too much for that. Even if she had seen the way he crossed his legs and that twitch in his eyes every time a certain female weather presenter came on their telly box.

How times and family ties had changed. Even though Connie and Ted hadn't. Other than age, their ways were pretty much fixed: a bit of a snack at 2.30 pm, nap till 4.30 pm, tea at 5, bed at 8 pm. She'd fall asleep into something funny and Irish. Wrapped in a cosy Maeve Binchy book. And he'd seem to drift off into the Alastair McLean one he'd had since last Christmas—fighting those German's into his dreams, endlessly the hero.

He would always be her hero.

'You can't teach an old dog how to meow,' Ted often said to the World, whilst making a cup of tea for them both.

Each time Connie would chuckle and whisper back: 'Or an old kittie to bark,' then she'd wink at him and make a small dog barking noise whilst pawing his hand that stirred their cups.

The waves of old age had battered their shores but they still felt like giddy kids half the time, inside at least. It was only when those pains came, standing up from the couch or they couldn't quite fix something, that each moment's decay and the pit of reality seemed to set in. It felt like all around them everything and everyone was getting more distant and all they had, regardless of the silly squabbles, was each other.

Co-dependents to the last lap. Bungalow buddies, she'd say.

They felt it coming. Sooner or later realty's bomb would drop.

Its ticking cast a shadow over those cups of tea and hid in the shaky TV reception as it occasionally flickered as the aerial blew in the wind. Ted kept saying he'd get up there and sort it out. Both of them knew it would never happen. It was a visual cue to their frailty and disconnect from modern ways: still not hard-wired to the relentless change in technology all around them.

Yes, the new shopping centre beckoned and to get a little something special for Ted, she thought and fiddled with the clasp on her little tartan purse. A gift from him to her last Christmas. He'd like that the silly old fool, a little pressie. He was silly, for putting her pants on her head when he was drunk. And a fool for loving her.

Yes, silly, old, fool—she loved him—to death.

To Death.

Connie's hands trembled with the purse clasp again, opening, checking. She inspected inside then snapped it shut with a cutesy little wry smile.

'Today's the day, finally. Now, let's go shopping.'

CONNIE HADN'T STOPPED smiling since she'd alighted the bus. Thanking the driver as always. It was the Brummy way. The city streets seemed the same as always to her, a tad busier maybe. A little buzz in the air, or maybe that was just her.

The shopping centre shone like a beacon to even more changes to come in the city. If the planners allowed this then anything could happen. This change she liked. A beaming new haven welcoming everyone in, parting with their hard-earned money and pensions. A glorious metal amorphous haven.

The shoplifters from the estates would be there too. Pushing the new security guards to earn their piece. The thieves would sprint down the tight little alleys and roads with their loot trailing and dropping behind them. So crass and clumsy, Connie thought. It was like they enjoyed the chase more than the loot. Connie was more subtle and understated in almost everything she did. Seeking out the simple glories and the smaller things of life.

She would take something. No chase. Her knees and legs weren't up to it.

With the absence of a real church in her World or a bowls club, hopes of shopping around the new centre were her true faith and calling: to potter, browse and mingle. Chat some extended small talk to a shop attendant that couldn't escape, then be home for a nap in front of the telly as usual. Murder She Wrote if Connie had the remote. Columbo, Lovejoy or the one with the detective in a wheelchair if Ted had it. Countdown if there was an unresolved squabble between them. And he'd assumed he'd got the last word in.

Seven letter word—boom, she'd say. Winner. Then, a cup of tea darling?

Debenhams department store called to her most of all amongst the shiny shops. A comforting, relatively unchanging safe place amongst the constant state of flux. The shopping centre may have a new glow but that shop would always be a familiar friend. A brand she warmed to as a child when her mother used to take her. And now, after she'd long gone. They would always be together walking those departments. New or not.

The doors opened for her by themselves; robotic curtains of the gods. Welcoming her and memories of her mum in. Her eyes widened as if she'd witnessed a miracle. Everywhere piles of gold like in a pharaoh's tomb. Fur and wool. Silk and lace. Pottery and china.

Smiling, she was in purest heaven. Shaking with anticipation of things she could never afford and on fantasies of how her life could have been. In another class. With another man.

She browsed the aisles like a drunk in a free bar. Intoxicated, giddy and jittering with excitement. She snuck into the underwear section like a shy nun, giggled and blushed at the frilly somethings that brought back vivid dirty memories; mainly from her first marriage. But, she had a plan to change that. They weren't dead yet. Had a pulse. And *it* still worked. She'd felt it sticking in her back when Ted was coming to most mornings in bed. That appendage always woke up half-hour before he did. It knew her body was there and was excited even if he'd grown used to the idea and just regarded it a bed warmer most of the time.

She picked up a little red lacy number. Visualised the evening. Held it a while feeling the silky texture as joyful hormones coursed through her veins.

She dropped it, as if it burned, then headed to menswear. Marching as if the spring in her step had been cut and replaced with a rod down each leg.

Tartan socks for him. Just how he likes them. Up to the knee and brushed material, soft, hardwearing and thick enough to absorb the smell for two days; unwashed. If he insisted on ignoring the washing basket as usual. Yes, he'd be happy with these ones, she thought. Stroked them like a kitten.

She just had a few more little bits to do before heading towards the till, which she did, bouncing along with all the love in the world.

'Having a nice day?' the cashier asked, unwittingly opening a tidal wave of bottled up small talk.

Connie could talk the bark off of a tree, Ted often said. A giant redwood at that.

'Yes, dear. So glad you've re-opened back up.'

The cashier looked worried. As if conversation wasn't part of her job description.

'It's hardly changed, really, has it?' Connie went on. 'I'm so happy to be allowed back in. You've done such a great job,' she said as if the shop assistant had single-handedly built the whole multi-million-pound development herself. 'Quite something.'

The young girl winced and looked around, it had been a complete overhaul in and out. All new staff too. The most expensive construction the city had ever seen, and likewise for the department store. Of course, Connie knew this— she just wanted interaction.

'I'm new.'

'The old staff got let go, did they? So sad, dear. Too tired looking and not up to the new sparkly image? I expect you're glad to get back to work anyway, dear, aren't you? Been getting bored at home watching Neighbours and Home and Away. Whatever you lot like these days.'

Again, the assistant looked as though she was burying frustration.

Corrie ignored it. 'I miss Kylie and Jason.'

The cashier shrugged. Looking at her as if she was on a school trip she didn't want to be on and the old lady was a museum exhibit, dropping echoes of the past that meant next to nothing.

The old lady was impervious to cynicism and full of shopping happiness and elated to be out mingling again.

'I've only just left school. Hadn't even worked before, not at all when I was given this one in the shop.'

'Yes, dear.'

'That was down to these, I think,' she cupped a tight breast in each hand.

Connie pretended she didn't notice, lost in her world.

'Have a nice day, dear,' Connie said as she walked away. Beaming, like a cat with keys to the creamery, and that special little something for Ted tucked neatly away out of sight. A surprise.

She sat on a bench outside and watched the pedestrians coming and going. Then she looked in her shopping bag and smiled to herself, so happy.

She could cry.

Looking up, the clouds seemed perfect, as did the pigeon pecking at crumbs by her feet. Everything was in its right place again. Ted would soon forget the rows and arguments they'd been having—everything was going to be okay.

But then… it wasn't.

Then, it happened.

A deafening noise. Glass flew: Utopia was shattered. Along with her hip, knees and windpipe. Her arm was ripped by steel as her hand held the shopping bag tight.

She wouldn't let go of her dreams for her and Ted before they burned.

ICU: Ward 9, Bed 3

'Who have we got in here then?' the doctor asked, picking up a clipboard from the end of the bed. Stains on the inside of the curtains pulled around them stood testament to tried and failed efforts to save the old dear's body on the now red patchy sheets dripping to the linoleum.

'It's another one. This ward's full, next door too,' the nurse said.

'Do they know the full picture yet? What actually happened?' the doctor asked.

'Nail bomb, maybe more than one. Set off simultaneously,' she whispered as her eyes welled up.

'Fuck. Have they caught the people who did it yet?'

'Don't think so… you know as much as me.'

'Just chatting to get by. You know the drill,' and he cast her a knowing glance. Like they were at war. Always on the front line bandaging life's casualties. 'Why do people do this shit? Everyone's quite capable of drinking, smoking and driving themselves to early death. They don't need to bother doing it to each other as well.'

They'd both seen it all. But still, she cried.

'We need to quieten down now,' the nurse whispered. Raising a hand and gesturing with her eyes over to the side.

He was used to it. Knew her looks intimately and was used to ignoring them. Most of the time.

A silhouette moved on the other side of the curtains which the doctor didn't seem to notice.

'Why do we need to be quiet? I don't think she'll be hearing anything anytime soon, nurse,' he waived at the body in the bed, 'In fact, I doubt she'll ever be doing much of anything ever again.'

A tear dropped from the nurse's cheek and mixed with a patch of blood on the floor.

The machines at the bedside stuttered on the doctor's words like they understood the futility of their efforts; pumping, beeping and feeding the bloody mass in the bed sustenance for those last few minutes... seconds... mere moments, before that final curtain call.

'No, not for her, doctor, We need to button it. Her husband's behind us. He just walked in.'

'Oh,' he said and put a finger to his own lips. Slowly closing his eyes as if to wish the shame away.

TED PARTED THE curtains like they were made of sheet steel. He hadn't left the house in weeks, too tired. Everything getting harder by the second. But, answering the door to those uniforms, getting to the hospital and now parting those curtains: it was all a series of the most difficult things he'd ever had to do in his whole life.

He looked at the body in the bed; Connie's body.

His life and love lay still, fading away from him forever. He looked to the bedside table where there was a bloody Debenhams bag. He could see a pair of socks she'd bought for him, with a receipt which he slowly picked out. 'Connie,' he whispered as his bottom lip quivered. Then he noticed them... a pair of red frilly knickers. They weren't on the receipt. 'Oh Connie, not again. Been shoplifting, pet?' he smiled, a little, and then started to cry. 'You silly bugger,' he stuttered. Hardly able to get the words out. He started to sob like he was that small boy again. Waiting outside the schoolyard for his parents that never came. There was no one to comfort him then, and no one anymore now. Connie was all he had left. Now that his daughter had gone too.

6

YOU HAVE A VISITOR

AS THE FATMAN entered the prison canteen, most of the room and everyone in it felt it: flexing, tensing and stiffening up. On a knife-edge. No introductions were needed. There was a wash of black. He walked as if on an executioner's march, proudly surveying the room to pick out his latest victim or to pick a couple of new axemen for his beck and call.

The guards cleared the room. All but two.

The only one's not seeming to notice were the two lads the Fatman had come to see. They were fixed in their own scheming. In tune with each other and communicating in mere gestures and odd words and glances.

Their attention would soon be fixed. Their own bomb was about to drop.

The lad's lives and minds were about to get bent out of shape. The Fatman's will was an unstoppable torrent. A wicked rich darkened river that carried the bodies of his past as it drowned those he met on his way.

'Lads, look up,' a guard slapped the table and they both looked up with daggers behind their eyes. The interruption had come as they sneered; high on scheming and games. The night before brought particularly bloody thoughts to resolve—like they all saw what was to come. They hadn't cared if everyone could hear them in the halls and cells then and didn't care much for the guard's hand on the table now.

'You have a visitor.'

'Who gives a fick,' Jake said and Pete giggled as he picked at some week-old ketchup from the tabletop like it was a juicy dried up scab then gnawed it from his fingernail.

'Unless they've tits like canons and a cock-thirst—we don't want to see them, sonny,' Pete said.

'Send 'em back where they came from,' 'Now get going, little piggy,' and Jake waved his hand at the guard like he was a fly on their last meal, 'Oink Oink. Trot on.'

'Go, now,' Pete echoed.

'You don't get to choose who you see, lads. This one least of all. Even I can't stop him.' The guard stared down at them. His eyes tore deep with a look of hate and an ounce of sheer pity. Like they were savage dogs waiting to be put down for ripping a child's face off.

'It's alright,' Jake said. 'One outta two ain't so bad,' he glanced up, 'Look—they've big fat titties after all. Jugs out, pet. Da boys are thirsty.'

They didn't care that the humour was misplaced. Like willing rats on a guillotine. Scrambling and dancing about the blade and headstock; enjoying playing with fire.

They glanced over at the Fatman as he neared the table with a thud-thud of authoritative boots. They were both used to the guards looking at them with hate and vengeful eyes. This big Fatman had something else: God's weakened attempt at forgiveness and the Devil's fury in every step.

He hadn't sat down yet. They liked him already.

Both automatically sat up. Bolt upright. Like it was a priest that had approached and they still gave a shit. They'd wandered off that path long ago and their alters' had been doused in blood ever since.

Maybe this Fatman in black was to christen them back into action?

'Boys, boys, boys… my sweet little boys,' the Fatman said and sat down on a flimsy chair that creaked in protest.

The guard made himself scarce as the Fatman reached over the table which creaked as well as it took the full weight of his mass. He grabbed hold of both their hands. Squeezed.

Their eyes narrowed. They flinched a little but didn't move away. Narrowing their eyes to a focus. There was a charge between the three men. They all felt it in the air. In those hands. Destiny and blood. Bound together in the glorious destruction to come.

'You a priest or summit?' Jake asked sarcastically. His eyes were like doubting windows to a mind that never trusted.

The Fatman cast a look at them—vengeful pity—as though life had been an open wound that never scabbed over. But still, they had kept picking at it.

'Executioner or lawyer? I'm going with…' Pete joined in.

The Fatman sighed. Let it hang in the air, then started his sermon: 'What I am, lads, is deliverance. Purpose.'

'Shite,' Pete said.

'Your new meaning.'

'Double-shite,' Jake sniggered, but they were both already sold—their expression changed to confirm it. The big man in front of them had a familiarity carried with him. Dead bodies on his heels around a wake of hurt. It was like he was family; an old friend. Truly a saviour… like they'd always known each other and always would. *Together forever.* All written into a story that circled round and round going everywhere and nowhere all at once. A Möbius strip.

'Do we know you, big man?'

'I know you, Jake. And you, Pete. I know what you've done. Where you're from.'

'Triple-shite,' Pete said, sounding as non-committal in doubting the Fatman as Jake.

Both were visibly eager—doubly sold. It was like they were around the Christmas dinner table winding up a relative. Thick as thieves. Hungry for pudding.

'And the best thing is lads, I know what you're going to do and where you're going.'

Their eyes narrowed again and their smiles followed. Not used to taking any sort of orders, their minds adjusted quickly, falling in line. This fitted. The big mass holding their hands carried with him the father figures they thrived for. The fire in his words and eyes lit them both up. They saw in him the evil retaliation on life they craved too.

'After we're done with our work boys. It'll be like you were never really here at all,' he looked around the room like it was crumbling to dust all about them. 'It'll be like you were nowhere. And everywhere. Fucking gods and martyrs to the masses. Carved in granite.'

They both slowly nodded. Waiting for the full weight of the deal to drop in their laps.

A dusty fluorescent tube flickered overhead and then decided to stay off.

'Annihilation. That's what you seek, yes?'

'Yes,' they chanted.

The Fatman reached into a bag and grabbed something book-sized in a dark red cloth and unwrapped it.

'First, meet your maker. Your saviour,' the Fatman put a copy of a book called Division on the table, turned to the author's bio page and squashed the book flat. Like he was a priest, after all, showing a sacred passage to the needy: the secret to existence and what awaited them in the afterlife. 'I influenced the library trolley a while back. Put some copies of this in your line of sight.

'Aye,' they both said.

'So?' Jake continued.

'I believe you know this man...' he stabbed with a world-worn stubby finger.

They looked down at the author's photo under the Fatman's digit.

'Aye, we know this army-fuck,' Pete said.

'Saved us you could say,' Jake muttered.

'He did nothing but put you in here. Didn't he? And just when you were on the steps of glory, boys, about to walk up and kiss Diablo on the cheek...' the Fatman said gravely. 'Hows about when you're out of here, you pick up where you left off—finish your business.'

'You mean...' Pete started.

'Bombs, sir?' Jake finished.

'Yes, boys, bombs,' the Fatman said, taking away his hand and letting the book slowly turn its own pages to hide the author's image again. A ghost. Never really there. 'And with it *he'll* be gone,' he slammed his hand on the book to hurry its pages shut.

The lads grinned hard as if their cheeks might split.

'The final insult is that he saved you from nothing, didn't he? He saved the victims from nothing too. He should have delivered you to the grave, let you take your martyrdom all those years ago.'

'Aye, sir.'

'It's what you wanted, yes? Deserved. Your rights.'

Jake: 'Yes.'

Pete: 'Yes.'

They nodded to the Fatman's sermon.

'I have a plan.'

'Big bombs?' Pete and Jake said together.

'Big bombs, boys. Yes.

'A show of strength,' Jake said.

'And what a bloody show it will be. What-a-show,' the Fatman gripped their hands on the table again and looked at the ceiling like it had been removed.

They joined him looking at the imagined sky. Sights on an afterlife. Getting there launched from life's torments on a rocket fired by an explosion that would rock the World—one fuelled by the blood of those blinkered to their struggles: slaughtered lambs to feed rabid dogs.

'Nails. Torn metal. Flames and flesh,' the Fatman said.

'Amen,' the lads said together.

'Boom,' the Fatman whispered and gestured with his hands.

'Amen,' the lads muttered.

7

RYAN AND BLACKWOOD

RYAN DID HIS military service with Blackwood in Afghanistan, Iraq and Ireland. Just to name a few. The Lost Years they said. Lost to war but sticking to their memories like hot tar to skin. That shit didn't come off and left a lasting impression. Scarred deep.

They went way back and missed it all really. Civvy life just wasn't the same.

Now, after all that war, working the doors of the main shopping centre in Birmingham city centre seemed a breeze. Both were well over experienced to be security guards, God help any shoplifters or chavs dicking-around on their watch. They loved the break from duty and the sense of authority, all without putting their necks on the line for a change. Child's play.

It was like a computer game they knew they'd have to turn off at some point soon.

As far as they were concerned they'd seen a ton of shit, had lived through it and probably shouldn't have. Therefore God was looking out for them. His dark angels, they'd decided. Their new roles were an easy vocation after all the blood, shit, war and worse they'd been through. It had hammered them like a butcher's mallet.

These new roles wouldn't be for life.

Now they looked to take the easy life, for a few more months, to re-calibrate before getting back to all the hurt. Eventually, they'd get some real work, as they called it. Find some heads to bash together for money. They had the experience and a thirst for dishing it out. Maybe they'd sign up to a more specialist security squad, for a private rich couple or go full-on mercs for hire abroad. For now, they were coasting: laying back, sipping on a latte and watching the young girls in tight dresses and tighter muffler pants shop for even tighter ones, hoping to give them a pat-down if they looked suspicious. And sometimes if they didn't. Sluts and hos the lot of them—they loved it.

Ryan and Blackwood were wolves.

There was this one girl who kept coming back. A dirty pretty little thing. Penny, Shaz, Trudes or something. They weren't all that sure. She kept getting caught by them on purpose. A shoe up her skirt, a bag hidden in another bag, a dress on top of a dress. She wasn't trying that hard to get away with it. By the end, she wasn't stealing anything at all. Just went up to them and said she'd been a naughty girl, needed a drilling. A sorting out and them some more.

They knew their duty, gave it to her. Out of sight.

They'd shoot the breeze in a dark security corridor with a flickering tube overhead. No one could get in, only they had the keys. They'd catch up on current events, memories of battlefields, glossing over the horror as always. All the while she'd be on her knees taking her morning's punishment. Her willing mouth and throat were full. Head bobbing eagerly. She'd finish one off and shuffle on her knees to the next.

Echoes of war far away. But always there.

She seemed to love it. Sometimes going straight back and starting over again with another round. Some days they loved it too. On most though, it was just part of the job; an unforeseen perk after all the shit life had pushed their way.

God owed them. That's how they saw it. They were his dark angels. Treading water before the bombs went off, again. They always did.

RYAN AND BLACKWOOD leant against the wall alongside the automatic doors to the shopping centre main entrance. Looking for the next eager victim and basking in a new day's sun as it bleached the concrete. They smoked. Thinking. Grinning. It was a hard graft but someone had to do it.

Their mock New York style policeman's outfits made them look like strippers, and their hard muscles underneath added perfectly to the image. They behaved more like bouncers than guards. After all, they'd been through. Life was sweet. Both pairs of eyes darted over the day's fresh waves of crowds walking past, in, out and towards them and the entrance to the shopping centre. Their domain. Prey.

'When are we gonna check back in, see how the other lads in the squad are?' Blackwood said, tapping the plastic lid to his disposable coffee cup before taking a sip.

'The ones that made it you mean?' Ryan took a sip of his own.

'You heard from any of them…any at all?' Blackwood insisted.

'Stevo's met a girl. Brian's a plumber, joiner or some other shit in Bristol. Weston-super-Nightmare or some shit hole. Mikey's the same, picked up a trade in God-knows-what.'

'Bollocks. What the fuck? What about Jimi?'

'Playing the guitar and bashing heads. ACDC covers I heard. They've all gone shite. For civvy bollocks.'

'You sure… Stevo's settled down, has he? Jimi the same?'

'Yeah, true, man. All fucking true.'

'Crazy, man. You mean that scary bitch in the bunker hole didn't put Stevo off the pussy after all.' 'Fuck me,' Blackwood whispered.

'Yep, He didn't go full-on gay after that—like we always said he would. And who would blame him.'

'The cunt nearly gelded him,' Blackwood whispered again.

'That was some fucking scary desert action. Hot sand and one scary assed bitch with a homemade knife. Going down holes to face up to banshees with razor-sharp tin lids. All that and you ain't supposed to fire back. What's that shit all about, man?' Ryan said.

'Too-true, Ryan. So fuckin-true. Didn't say anything about battering them with a two by four though did it? Makin' it look like the roof fell in,' Blackwood smirked into his cup.

'How many stitches did Stevo get in his ball sack again?'

'About twenty. Put the first two in myself. Stopped his nuts dropping out waiting for the medevac team. Was tempted to put a stitch in his bell-end too whilst I was down there. Cheeky fucker.'

Both sniggered, spurted coffee out onto the warm paving. It was a hot day and only going to get hotter.

They both started into a full-on laughter fit. They had to. It was all true.

It was the stories they couldn't talk about, the ones in their dreams that woke them each night and made them jump when a door slammed. They were the real problem. It's why they laughed now. If they didn't they'd cry. There was a lot of blood when their pal Stevo had his scrotum half removed down that bunker hole. A river of it. That was the last image neither of them mentioned or talked about. Omitting the hard truths:

rivers of black blood, soil and sand mixing together. All impossible to get off their hands or out of their minds.

A singular cloud moved in front of the sun, giving everyone a moment's respite as if the world blinked in a pause for thought. A stark reminder that whatever the light, darkness would always come next. Always.

'This is all right, isn't it?' Ryan said, sounding unsure.

'Aye, maybe we should coast along like this forever? We don't need any more blood back in our lives, do we?' Blackwood sounded unconvinced as well.

They were both married to a certain way of life. They knew their calling. That the civvy life was a blip.

'You'd miss it wouldn't you? If we left the hard graft for good,' Ryan said.

'How come?' Blackwood shrugged.

'The lawlessness of war. You're a fucking cowboy at heart, man.'

'You getting fucking philosophical on me now, Ryan?'

'Just mean you could, or we could do what we fucking wanted going forward. Like now. The way we are, we don't have to be enlisted. Just like, you know...remember that boy and his family on the road back to the 5th that time?' Ryan grinned. It was a dark image they'd never spoken of since. Didn't need to. But now it fitted. Highlighted what they could get away with.

'Seem to remember you took a bit of meat and disposed of it after too, Ryan,' Blackwood feigned a formality that would never really exist between them. They'd always be the same rank. High or low.

There was a pause. Stillness in the air.

A group of teenage girls approached with tiny tight dresses, crop tops and make-up like they were of legal age. Not that that mattered to either of the men.

'Check this lot out,' Ryan said.

'Hell yes, man. That's exactly what I'm talking about. Tell me, these have been bad girls,' Blackwood touched the zip on his trousers, undoing it a little and closed his eyes to imagine them in a line in the security corridor.

'Please, God, please. We deserve this,' Ryan said. Just as an old lady carrying a Debenhams back walked slowly in front of the girls and spoiled the view for them.

'Shit it,' Blackwood said, peering through one eye.

'Still, it's pretty easy this, isn't it? This life? Maybe we could still take more of what we wanted? Join another crew, form one ourselves,' Ryan said.

'You really don't want to put your feet up, do you? Go full civvy?'

They turned their heads and looked at each other. Stared hard, pretending to be serious. Glaring each other down. It lasted only thirty seconds then they cracked up and returned to staring at the pedestrians. Letching at the girls.

'Nah,' they both said together. Deep inside wishing they were different people. Sat on a beach, sipping cocktails; feet in the sand and without a care.

'Hell no,' Blackwood finished and his eyes widened as if smelling the gunpowder to a shot that was to kill him.

Something wasn't right.

Then, it happened.

They felt it deep inside, like a sixth sense, having been to war. The rumble came, then a fierce roar. God's answers to their horrid prayers. Like a mountain top had blown off and they were about to be turned to stone.

In one blast all of their memories fused as one.

An explosion. Splinters of glass, wood, shards of stones falling. An instant of flame all around them, clouds of smoke, dust and debris.

Then nothing.

It settled as suddenly as it had started. Like God had been eavesdropping and answered their innermost wants defiantly. Had heard every word and seen every sordid action and then decided to decline their requests. Instead, turning the world to black and everything in it to dust on the floor. A blanket over them.

'Man down, man down!' Ryan said, his voice muffled over the reverberations and ringing in his ears. Barely getting the words out. There was a dying heavy mass on top of him.

It was Blackwood.

ICU: Ward 10, Bed 2

'Another one?' the doctor asked, picking up a clipboard from the end of the bed and looking at the dead-tired nurse. It had been a long day turned into an endless night.

'His friend's outside. Desperate to get in and see him.'

'Well, he'll have to wait a little longer. Need to plug this one up some more. Needs more blood. Make the call now, nurse. He won't last the night.'

'They're both ex-military. Active service all over the World. Sounds hard.'

'Been through all that shit and a fucking nail bomb takes you out in Birmingham.'

'Life's a bitch,' the nurse said and the doctor nodded slowly. They knew it more than most. 'The one in the bed saved the one outside. Threw himself on him when the blast went off.

That's why he's bleeding out in the bed and his pal is outside crying for the first time in his life.'

'Fuck me…Let the lad in.'

'Thank you.'

'Why?'

'I don't think he's got anyone else. They just had each other.'

RYAN LOOKED AT his friend in the bed. The room, hospital, nurse and doctors were just white noise—nothing else mattered. Just these last moments. Louder in silence than the bomb that had put them there.

He knew he was going soon. Blackwood wouldn't last the night and Ryan wanted to see what was left of him, the man that saved him, one last time. Like he hadn't enough already.

On the side table were Blackwood's things: a wallet, a scrunched up brochure for a holiday and a booking confirmation on a flight. Two seats: *Mr F. Blackwood and a Mr C. Ryan.*

'Stupid bastard,' Ryan muttered. 'You should be here. I should be the one checking out. Not you… Not. You.'

Stapled to the holiday booking was a scratch card, not a massive win, but enough. Scrawled on the back:

We Deserve This Ryan—No More War.

8

GHOSTS

A TREK IN Borneo's jungles was what John and Cherry needed. They opted to go without a guide. It was their adventure and didn't want every tree, ape and snake pointed out to them. They wanted to discover it themselves. All of it, alone, with the elements and with everything the jungle had to offer.

A rough river tributary started the trail with a fallen tree as a bridge over vicious rapids. Cherry and John bounced over rocks and boulders on the river bed towards it. A welcome challenge to start the trek; a bridge into the undergrowth.

They travelled light. Nothing but t-shirts, shorts and trainers on and a water bottle to share. Coming the other way on the other side of the waters were a small group of over-prepared German tourists. Unmistakable as their accents snapped on the jungle breeze like marching orders and a barking abrasion to anything that attempted to trivialise their formalities. They were heavily laden, complete with hiking boots, rucksacks, maps and compasses and looked unnecessarily panicked as they neared John and Cherry.

'We're turning back,' the front one yelled. 'The trail's too rough,' and they hobbled hesitantly over the fallen tree over the water's rapids towards the other side where Cherry and John were standing.

Both were puzzled by the group; equipped for adventure, but without the verve. The rapids beneath the Germans crashed around rocks and the upturned roots from the tree, and they climbed down the other side, one by one, and looked John and Cherry up and down. Disapprovingly. Like teachers to a pair of truant kids caught smoking—*Tut. Tut.*

'You're going into the jungle…dressed like that?' the last woman climbing down from the tree roots said.

'Yes,' Cherry said. 'We'll be okay.'

'Seriously?'

'We'll be fine. Don't worry,' Cherry put a foot up to start climbing.

'You silly English,' one of the men in the group said.

The waters splashed up and the jungle swayed as big black birds flew overhead.

The group looked a little closer at the pair and started to notice details. Skin deep. Those black eyes. And the scars on John's arm and leg…Then, the *Who Dares Wins* tattoo.

They started to quietly nudge each other. Muttering.

'Seriously, we'll be fine,' John said and gestured at Cherry as she crested the roots of the tree at the start of the crossing and started over the tree bridge.

She turned around and held her hand down to pull him up in a mutual show of co-joined strength.

The Germans stared on as the pair crossed without looking back.

On the other side, the edge of the trees beckoned John and Cherry in as the jungle woke with calls of strange wild birds and other animals in the distance. John loved the excitement and knew she did too.

He was reminded of his training all those years ago and behind him now, as much as the gangs and criminals that had brought him and Cherry together. Now they could leave it in the past and walk into the wilds of the jungle together, free. Breaking ground on a new trail as they went.

John bent down and picked up a stick shaped like a gun. Turned to Cherry and then threw it into the undergrowth. Images of yesteryear were disregarded. He did still pick it out and see it as something else. That visibly bothered him. That it wasn't—just a stick.

'Do you think we'll see any snakes? An orangutan?' she asked, changing the focus. And she looked up above them through the huge canopy of trees. The sun streamed as it caught the silhouettes of insects, webs and falling leaves as if caught in mid-air.

'Anything with any sense will have clocked us, and hidden, long before we catch a glimpse.'

'But it was so noisy as we entered? Now it's so still.'

'Peaceful. Could really lose ourselves here.'

'Hope so.'

They already had…in a moment.

But, nothing lasts.

A crack of a broken branch up ahead broke their moment and reminded them they were still on the tourist trails and not quite hidden from the reality they looked to escape. The occasional litter they started to notice confirmed the illusion was shattered.

Clump. Clump. Came the noises of footsteps approaching. Heavier than most.

A large man that they half recognised approached. He was about as prepared as they were, by the German hiker's standards, travelling irresponsibly light.

The man approaching was sweating like only a man his size could. He carried a water bottle in bloodied hands.

It looked like he'd fallen or caught them on a branch. Bits of leaves and twigs stuck to his wrists.

'Alright there?' came an American accent carrying a surface deep greeting. His eyes looked as though they were scrutinising them. His mouth faked a forced smile. Cracking his sweaty face. Different from the German's, his look was full of distaste. Then, it changed to something much colder. He passed them by, without another word or a glance, clumping off with his heavy legs and feet.

It was like a reaper had beat them to it. Taken its wildlife, heart and soul. Silencing the jungle in a wash of black.

'What the fuck was that?' Cherry said. 'It's normally the other way around isn't it? People are disappointed to see Americans everywhere they go. Like they're invaders. He looked at us as if we were spoiling *his* view.'

'Maybe he didn't like us witnessing him turning back either, defeated, like the other lot. Or, he just wanted the place to himself?'

'Cut himself a little. Did you see?'

'Yes,' John said. He could tell when someone was bothered by their own or others' blood. The big American wasn't. He wore it like his sweaty black T-shirt. As if it was part of his outfit for the day. Dead natural. He didn't hide it. Wanted people to notice. 'Disappointed the jungle wasn't his—just like us now.'

It was an easy call. To say it was a tourist rivalry thing. Everyone wants to be there first, fresh footprints in the leaves. Be the first to break new soil. Knowing: nothing's that pure anymore.

They both felt it. There was something else in the large American's eyes and the blood on his hands. He'd looked at them like they were a known enemy. Like he was measuring them for a coffin.

The stillness broke with a distant cry. Then another. A now-familiar set of rustlings in the trees and a call of an exotic bird, then another and another. Welcoming them back in. Their own senses switched from the passing encounter back to the nature around them. A massaging harmony.

For now, the jungle was theirs again.

'Back in the room,' she said.

'The jungle is ours,' he replied.

And for now, it was. The Fatman hadn't taken it from them. Yet.

THE FATMAN TRUDGED up the jungle path. Sweating buckets. He'd done his time in hot sweaty jungles and could have resented this one. But it was worth it. The prize. Each step brought him close to a sick release in tormenting others. And a pot of cash that meant he could hand the damn badge in for good. Figuratively speaking. Of course, he'd keep it. It opened too many doors and dropped a coachload of knickers. He'd never give that card up. The true gift in the proceedings was the theatre of it all and evil mind games. He loved it. It made his life, and this jungle trek, more than worth it.

Up ahead a monkey screeched and then an exotic-sounding bird call followed.

'Daddy's coming,' the Fatman whispered. 'Daddy's coming,' he took a swig from his bottle then spat it at a tree like a cobra spitting venom through savage teeth.

The monkey silenced. Alarmed by a bloodthirsty predator. Wilder than most.

The Fatman stopped, looked back. He knew they'd be following him into the trees, following him up the path soon. The previous night's eavesdropping had given him the lead.

Their loved up whispers and touches had made him sick then. And the memory of it, in the jungle, made him dry retch. Heaving bent over. *Love hurts*, he thought. Wiping his mouth and standing back up. *To have to bare fucking witness to it.*

He took another swig from his bottle of water then held it up to the light streaming through the canopy of branches and leaves overhead as he imagined the next few hours and how it would shatter their loved up bubble. Like dropping a bomb into a schoolyard. They wouldn't see it coming— nowhere to go. They'd take the full blast face on.

He walked on and the trees seemed to bend around him.

'Distorted truths,' he said to no one but himself. 'Lost in a matrix of fate.'

He stopped and held up his hand again. Through the lens of the bottle's water, he could see a blurred orange figure appear in the trees, stretching from a high up branch, then stopping as it noticed the Fatman.

'You'll do,' the Fatman said, lowering the bottle to see the ape eye to eye. It was as if they both knew it was a turning point. They were frozen, staring. Knowing that the next move would be final.

He slowly reached for the Glock with a silencer tucked in his belt.

'Yes, you'll do nicely—my endangered orange friend. Very nicely indeed.'

Thud-Thud.

Snap. Crunch.

THEY STARED. Then she cried as he began to well up too.

They'd both grown a distaste for humans and with it grew an increased respect for nature. His Viking roots had become more and more apparent as their time and bond together had evolved. He was a pagan at heart, attuned to the ebbs, flows and washes of the seasons with the animals and creatures alongside him. She was now too.

The sight before them was more criminal and evil than most they'd seen.

An ancient tree's base was soaked in blood. The jungle floor's leaves and sticks were speckled with more blood about it. When whoever had done this had finished, they'd sat the orangutan's body up, facing the path so everyone would see.

'A local making a statement…A tourists go home thing?' Cherry stuttered.

'This is something else,' John looked at the beautiful creature. Its image and body now defiled. 'That American—a trophy hunter maybe?'

'Really?' she didn't sound as if she wanted to believe it.

He knelt down, noticing its mouth ajar. 'There's something in it.' He pulled out a bloody folded newspaper clipping from the orangutan's mouth, unravelled it as the dead ape stared blankly back at him. A knowing look; sympathy from nature's dead witness.

'What is it?' she said.

'A clipping. I've seen it before.'

She looked at the piece of paper in his hands as they started to tremble. The bloodied sheet held all of their histories, paths and futures as they coalesced in a singular faded image of two boys, now men, in borrowed suits and the headline:

EVIL BOMB PLOT BOYS RELEASED EARLY.
WHAT'S NEXT FOR JUSTICE?

'The lads you didn't shoot?'

'And then got court-martialled for it... The very same.'

'Fuck,' she said.

'A little older now.'

'Don't look like they should be out.'

'Worse than when they went in,' he saw the same fire in their eyes.

She looked, the image burned past the blood-stained tabloid sheet and photographers attempt to frame some redemption.

John walked a few steps into the undergrowth and knelt on his knees. He closed his eyes slowly and drew a symbol in the soil by his knees with his fingers. The Viking symbol for the Matrix of Fate:

He opened his eyes again and started to dig into the symbol with his hands. Slowly at first then quicker. She joined him.

They had a big hole to dig. A grave. It would be big enough to hold the body of the great ape, alongside any hopes they'd had of escaping his past.

In the shadows of the undergrowth, a bloodthirsty tiger watched and waited.

It was nearly time.

9

LILLY AND STELLA

THE GIRLS HAD both grown up, played and skipped school together for years. Now, fifteen years old, they dressed to look older. To get what they wanted. They knew they could pass for twenty-one, easily. Lilly's tits and Stella's legs distracted most boys from the boring details of milestone birthdays anyway. Instead, they measured life by the quick cheap fixes instead; anywhere and when they could get them. Ciders and gropes, they said to each other before they set out. It's that simple. They knew it worked and how to use what they had. They had no interest in schoolwork, only boy's…and men.

Sometimes they just wanted each other. When they were messing around in the graveyard, experimenting: Cider Games they called that. 'A filthy sin,' the priest had renamed it. When he'd caught them; fingers wet, mouths drooling. He didn't interrupt their game until after he'd finished doing his own dose of self-gratification; peeping like a pervert from behind the trees and bushes.

The girls knew he was there. Letching. And liked it. It got them off even more. Added to the kick.

Now, their explorations had moved on, they'd evolved, deeper. Now they wanted men more than boys. They were predators on a fast track to a lifelong financial sponsorship in early pregnancy as they saw it. It was a single mum, working-class wisdom passed down from generation to generation.

Nothing would stop them.

'Older men. With some experience.' Lilly said and licked the tip of the flavoured lip gloss before applying it to her mouth.

'For a pounding,' Stella said. 'That *is* what we need.'

'A squaddie on shore leave.'

'Or, some sex-starved security guards,' Stella said back and looked at the two new security beefcakes leaning up against the shopping centre entrance, smoking. Leering out. Oozing predatory laddishness. The girls loved it.

'I've been there a few times. With them both. They're alright.'

The men weren't the only hunters out and about. There were two more predators on the streets that day. Their armour was short and tight-fitting.

'Not bad. Danny Dyer on steroids. Yours, on the left, is more a footballer sort.'

'I fucking love Danny Dyer. We could swap at half-time if you like.'

They laughed, getting wet at the thought of it, together.

'I know, pet... look... I think we're on,' Lilly smiled and winked in the guards' direction. The men looked back and one of them played with his fly suggestively.

The girls almost got closure in eye contact, sealed the deal, but an old lady got in the way and spoiled the view. Just as they were going to pull their tops down a bit, flash a bit of leg too. Finish it with the wink. It never failed. But, the fucking blue rinser killed the mood.

Stella finished rolling a second fag. One for her, one for Lilly. She fumbled with the papers back into her purse.

Then it came. A bigger mood killer. Shaking the ground they stood on.

Flying shards of glass cut across Stella's face then came the sound of the ear-splitting blast. A shower of smaller fragments hit the concrete and car and shop alarms went off together in harmonious despair.

The rollie Stella was about to hand to Lilly lay on the floor with two of her fingers separated from the hand they were from. Immaculate red fingernails as red as the blood they rested in.

Lilly convulsed on the floor, in shock and pain. Nails, glass and bits of shop window frame were in her legs and stomach. She lay on her side, twitched and looked at her best pal, her friend for life: Stella.

Friends till the end, now it came. Fading out.

She wanted to see her one last time. But, Stella didn't have a face anymore.

ICU: Ward 17, Bed 21

'Why weren't they in school?' the doctor said.

'You never bunk off, Doc'?' one of the nurses said.

'No,' he said coldly.

'Of course not,' the other nurse said and shook her head. 'Such a waste. How old were they, seventeen… eighteen most.'

'They were fifteen. Should have been in class,' The doctor hit the clipboard.

'Fuck,' they all said and shook their heads.

'Doc'?'

'Yes.'

'Can you speak to the parents outside? And, there's been this other guy hanging around as well. Thought he was a reporter or something. Has some agency badge. U.S. I think. Eagle and stars all over it.'

'I'll speak to the parents and get rid of the leach.'

'Everyone's all together in the Bad News Room.'

'We still calling it that?'

'I would have called it the Blue Room,' another nurse said and picked up the loose fingers off the bed sheet and put them in a plastic tub. On the bedside table was an Ann Summers bag that fell open. A couple of lacy and rubber things rolled out. And a card.

'I guess they'd picked those out to try together whilst waiting for the right men to come along?' a nurse said and glared at the Doctor.

'They never do,' another nurse said. 'The right ones... never do.'

The doctor retreated outside into the corridor. He knew the nurses would be talking about him, sharing stories. None of them good.

10

PANGKOR LAUT

AS THE SMALL boat bounced over the last few waves and hit the jetty, silhouettes of the island's structures stood out against the stillness of the sea in a glaring moonlight that looked like a perfectly circular window cut through to another time and place.

It was as close to Heaven on earth as they thought possible.

Large wooden hotel suites on stilts jutted out into the sea from sweeping walkways and gantries lit up by lanterns. The wooden walkways connected bandstands, yoga areas, pools and bars. Hammocks hung, swinging from the trees. Inviting them in.

They'd booked the resort a touch out of season so the island was only half occupied and they'd have most of the areas and staff to themselves. With the company of the local monkeys, hornbills and monitor lizards.

'Quite something,' John said.

'Perfect,' she agreed.

The Malay man piloting the boat cut the engine with a snap, grabbed their luggage and leapt to the jetty in one fluid, well-practised motion. Passing the bags to someone who was waiting on the jetty and ushered them off the boat. They were led down the dark wooden walkways on stilts over the sea. Their plane had been delayed; they'd missed their connection and got stuck in Abu Dhabi for a night in what felt like an oven. This left them to eventually approach the luxury island, seven hours late, in this the blackest of nights on a small taxi boat from the mainland. The porters and welcoming staff did their best to big up the newlyweds' arrival but they were tired too and had been kept up after a long day's graft, preparing the island, tending to the other guests. They were too broken in to welcome the pair with their usual ceremonial gusto. They did their best in a ritualistic greeting that was expected of the five-star island resort. It was clear everyone just wanted to sleep. Including John and Cherry.

They walked behind the porter and looked over the edge of the wooden walkways, down at the sea, beach and the tree lines nearby as large black shadows moved and shifted eerily on the boulders below.

'Resting monitor lizards absorbing yesterday's sun from the rocks,' the porter said without needing to look back at the couple or shapes on the rocks.

Troops of monkeys watched from the tree line as well, with pairs of eyes reflecting in the moonlight, as wild boar scurried and snuffled below the walkways waiting for scraps.

John and Cherry got to the end of the wooden walkway to their suite. It was set apart from the rest of them on stilts over the water. As if they were separated and singled out. It suited them fine.

The porter had the keys ready, unlocked and opened the wood panel door and it creaked open. He quickly began to hurry about his duties, knowing they were dead tired. He didn't dwell on the rose petals now in tepid bath water in the infinity room with open walls out to sea that must have must have been picture perfect seven hours ago. The towels folded into swan had also drooped and flopped to one side as more rose petals on the bed had long since wilted.

The romantic illusions had faded. But the whole escape from reality was already gone. It had been shattered days ago by the dead orangutan and newspaper clipping left for John and Cherry to find in Borneo. A fan turned slowly overhead and all three paused in the room. John and Cherry from layers of Jetlag. The porter waited tiredly and not-so-subtly for a long-overdue tip and to be excused to his quarters.

John obliged and the porter left their key on the side and walked out. Not before telling them to keep the doors locked, even when they were in—that the monkeys would steal anything, loved cameras and sunglasses and they bite.

'The romance is dead.'

'A biting feral monkey not do it for you?' John said and picked up a stale sandwich from a platter on the side, inspecting it.

'Maybe, monkey-boy,' she said.

John walked to the large open square bathroom area with open walls out to sea and looked out of the side that faced the shore. It was like they'd borrowed the imagery from someone else's dream.

He threw the sandwiches out one by one and they fell twenty feet to the sand below. Pensive shadows emerged from the treeline and zig-zagged across the sand. Snorting. Snuffling.

'Did you really just do that?' Cherry laughed.

'What…throw some stale sandwiches out? Yes, I did. And I'm starving too.'

'No, I meant—feed processed ham sandwiches to them.

'So…?'

'They're wild boar.'

'Oh,' John saw the distaste in his actions. Winced a little. 'The romance is definitely dead now.'

'You'll give them a taste for pig. Their own flesh. That can't be good.' Cherry undressed and lay on the bed.

John looked at the stars and moon reflecting off the sea again. An empty endless horizon going on forever. Behind them, and their rooms, it was as if the other resort suites and lights weren't there at all. It was like they were there alone. Between the flights, taxis, travelling and delays, he'd stopped clock-watching in the car ride to catch the ferry boat.

He looked at her on the bed and unbuttoned his shirt. Time stood still, would wait.

'Are we safe here?' she said moving from under him to be on top.

He said nothing—she knew the response. It too would wait.

11

WRITTEN IN SKIN

THE BIG AMERICAN charged down the hospital corridors like a drunk rhino. Trolleys spilled as nurses were barged as visitors and patients stared at him. He stopped for a moment, surprisingly not looking that out of breath to those who saw the size of him and the rate he'd moved.

He took out his mobile and stabbed at it with chubby fingers then lifted it to his face. 'They're bringing them in, Will. Or, the bits of what's left anyway,' he said into it.

'You won't find out any more than you know already running around that hospital. It'll be spilt over the papers tomorrow anyhow. Might as well step back. We don't want the Brits knowing we were anywhere near this one. The case is toxic. We made it so, knowing it was going down and did nothing...' the voice down the phone said.

'Just the way it is, Will.'

'Remind me again, big man. Why did you let it run its course— what's the big picture?'

'There are reasons much more than us and the dead,' he lied. It was only for him.

'Not sure you'll have done much for U.S. and U.K. relations if they get a whiff of it.'

The big man was tired, let out a sigh and hung up. Being an agent on home turf was soul-destroying enough, but doing it abroad with these Limey fucks really got his goat. He hadn't got what he deserved by his reckoning. Not one iota. Not yet.

He had a plan. Hell, it had already started.

Ever since he discovered these Paddy bombers were due to be released back onto the streets. He helped them in planning the job and visited them inside. It was inevitable, he made sure of it—as soon as they got out. All this and he wanted the world to know, the victims' families and friends to know most of all: those Paddy-bombing-pricks were only drawing breath because of one man's in-action: John Black. He hadn't taken the shot when he was ordered to and so the Paddies ended up locked up in a cell above ground, running some modest sentence when they should have been dead and buried boxed up underground.

The Fatman had made sure it had all fallen into place, and with those lads now blown to bits by their own hands, he just needed a sponsor or two—to finance his cause.

He'd pour the blame onto John Black for not taking that damn shot in Ireland all those years ago.

The big man flashed his ID card around like he was back home. It still worked. Still opened doors. Always would. America was the World police whether the World liked it or not— he fucking loved the power of that little card.

Maybe he'd use it to get a nurse to suck him off on the way out?

'Where are the Irish lad they've just brought in?' he barked at a desk, waving his ID card around again.

'Down the hall second left. It's a bit messy in there, you might want to gown up,' the girl on the hospital wing desk said, but he was already gone. Grinning all the way to the bloodbath.

'HOW MANY VICTIMS?'

'Who are you? Press?'

The doctor and nurses didn't look up as they retracted an IV line, rolled it up and hung it on a trolley, then put the plastic sheet over the lad's head.

The big man waved his card around again, enough for them to see the eagles and official feel of it if they bothered to look. It could have been a scrap of paper— no one paid it any attention and the Fatman's ego felt it.

'I'm part of the investigation,' he weighed in heavily.

'A yank interest. Feels complicated already.'

'It's less complicated now they lost their political affiliations. They were just crazed nihilists out to burn the world and everyone in it,' the Fatman said. Probably too much but he liked to show he knew more than anyone else in the room why they had all ended up in it, covered in blood.

'They always had an appetite regardless of the masthead I guess. Bitterness rising. Was gonna pop at some point. If only someone had got to them sooner. Had taken them out on their own instead.'

'Without anyone else getting hurt,' a nurse joined in.

'Funny you should say that,' the big man muttered.

'What?' the doctor asked, turning to look at a big American shadowing the room with his mass and mind.

The Fatman man knew John Black had the chance, to take the fucking shot. Never did. Now he loved to drop it into people's conscience—to sow the seeds of hate.

Blood dripped from the lad's body under the sheet. It pooled on the bedside then started to drop to the floor by the Fatman's feet.

'Excuse me,' a nurse said and moved the American back a step so she could deal with it. As she brushed past the bed a tattooed arm fell out. The big man looked, initially puzzled then his eyes widened. A smile followed.

'Bingo, mother fucker. Bing-go!' he snapped out his phone and took a photo,' it was priceless. A gift. Just what he needed.

'What do those mean? The words?' the nurse said, holding the arm that had fallen out and reading tattoos out: 'Untethered, Transference, Division,' her eyes looked confused.

The doctor leant around the bed end, pausing his filling out of the clipboard and time of death and joined her in looking at the boy's arm.

'Just some names they'd been trying for the World destroying nihilist thing they had going on.'

They could have used a pencil and paper if they were gonna change their minds about it,' the doctor said.

One of the nurses sniggered. An obviously involuntary reaction forced—all in the room were desperate for some light relief.

Not the big man. He was on a roll. He wasn't jaded or confused. The tattoos were a perfect set piece for him. Now to show them around. To put that last nail in John's coffin.

Back outside in the corridor, the Fatman leant up by a fire extinguisher and grinned to himself as he searched his smartphone. And there it was, confirmation. It was beautiful. The search results listed out with John Black's author profile.

The lad's had done well. The Fatman couldn't have carved into their flesh and the proceedings any better himself.

'Should have stayed in the SAS Johny-son,' the big man thought out loud and clicked through the links looking at John's background and author bio' pics.

A trolly with another body wheeled past with another nail bomber on.

'You really should have taken that shot, John.'

The trolly bounced along, the front right wheel struggling to straighten itself.

'You dumb fuck...hell, you should have taken two,' he smiled again looking at the trolly forced along carrying the second lad. He glanced into his phone as it glowed back in his face with photos of the Lad's tattooed arm again. He saw riches and poetic justice and all its glory. Now, the deed was done and the bomb had taken its victims. Now he could use the photo and the connection to John to drum up some interest. Those sponsors were going to cough it all up. He was due a final payout.

'Goodnight sweetheart,' he said coldly to the trolley as it disappeared around a corner.

The Fatman continued surfing on his phone. Scrolling news articles. His face smiled so hard his mouth might rip as he found what he was looking for. He looked at an article:

HISTORY RE-WRITTEN:
Disgraced SAS soldier ditches gangland ties to become a crime noir writer. Too dirty-real for some.

'John-lad, there's more to that headline isn't there,' the Fatman thought out loud, 'but, it'll fucking do. What about the finding love bit too though, eh?' he knew the victims' friends and family wouldn't look too kindly on the guy who'd failed to take out the nail bombers all those sorry years ago. Now with his happy, settled-down writer's life and a new wife. The families and friends would fucking hate that more than anything.

He saved a screenshot of the article and one pretentious mugshot of John from his publisher's page: a black and white one as he looked to an imagined horizon, puzzled.

The Fatman had all the bartering and emotional leverage he needed now in generous supply. That and his precious little ID card—it was going like a dream: a blood-oiled nightmare.

'Now, where are those weeping open wallets hiding?' he said and set off back down the corridor towards the lady at the desk again.

'The grieving room, pet. Where is it?'

She pointed from the desk without looking up.

He eyed John's photo on his phone screen as he walked away. 'Johnny-son, I always take the fucking shot. Whether I'm asked to or not. You're done. And your fucking squeeze.'

A hurrying nurse bumped into him, scurrying to stem another bleeding victim.

She'll do for later, he thought. 'You're going down, John. And she can too,' he smiled at his own wordplay.

Ten Years ago
CUBA. Art Haven Retreat grounds.
Special Agents' raid (1990s):

'BYRON, YOU'RE GONNA be a big man one day you keep eatin' like that,' Jed said checking the straps on his vest.

'Do you know what my name means?' Byron said back at him and loaded another bite of burger into his mouth and three cartridges into the pump-action all with the same hand. 'It means a barn for cows.'

'What the fuck?' Jed said and double-checked his Sig Sauer was clean and clear.

'And, when all this dirty work is finished…' he pointed past the car they were behind, up the dusty drive to the big farm building, now an artist's commune for societal drop-outs.

'Yes?'

'I intend to have my feet up on a desert island and be the size of a fuckin' cow in a barn. Basking like a walrus. Not giving a fuck'

'It's good to dream.'

'It's happening, Jed, one way or another,' he looked at Jed's Sig like it was a water pistol—totally harmless. Like he knew something about it.

'Not on these wages, Byron. No chance,' Jed was too busy to notice Byron scrutinising his weapon.

Byron nodded. 'Right-right you are. We need an extra way to get money. Government salary is shit.'

'Fact,' Jed checked the Sig again. He was obsessed with it. It had never let him down.

'I might have a few ideas,' Byron said. 'Ways to get paid twice on a job.'

'Watcha mean?' Jed straightened his arm and looked down the sights.

'Well, we're paid to be here and carry out a certain duty by the government, the agency, take down whoever the puppet masters say. Yes?'

'Yes. We are definitely here,' Jed shrugged.

'Well, what about the victims? Friends and family of those here. If you asked them for a special service on top of what we're already paid? To make sure you took the shot. Could even say the dept' didn't want us to. Even though we know we're gonna take it anyway.'

'Been meaning to talk to you about that, Byron...'

'Meaning what?'

'That hairpin trigger of yours. It's getting harder to write up. We can plant only so many guns. And make up the paperwork. It'll catch us up one day. You fucking know it.'

'Why have they put us on this raid, Jed?

'Why?' Jed sounded defeated. He looked at Byron like a bull that wouldn't move out the road.

'I'll tell ya what they put us on these shitty jobs— to take the fuckin' shot— that's why.'

'Fuck knows. Maybe. We're not assassins.

'Really?'

'Yes, man, fuck sake…chances are they're just gonna cry like babies in there. Not exactly gonna come at us with paint brushes and easels, are they? Fuckin' harmless saps.'

'I'm here… you're here… we're fucking here… because they know—we always—take—the damn shot. AND we, and them, don't ask about later. Right up the fucking paperwork, Jed, it's shredded anyway.'

SMOKE BILLOWED OUT the windows of the barn from the grenades and flashbangs. Screams came from inside. Panic.

Inside, upstairs, a girl whimpered in one of the bedrooms as Jed bled out the floorboards of a corridor. Byron looked at his Sig Sauer that he'd put the blanks into when Jed took his last leak before the raid.

'Sorry, Jed.'

Jed bubbled blood from his mouth. Looking confused. Angry. But mainly in complete disbelief as life started to fade from his eyes.

'Thing is. I've already got paid twice for this job.' Byron whispered in his ear, 'The agency who got us to do the raid paid up. And, the parents of the artist hippie girl you needlessly killed. Well, they wanted payback as well.' he looked to the bedroom where a girl whimpered.

Jed's eyes widened one last time—hatred.

'It's that sweet new gig I wanted to talk to you about—you shoulda listened, Jed.'

'What girl?' Jed bubbled and a tear welled then fell. Jed's trigger finger had never been light. Never excessive force. Over and over, all intentional kills. No needless casualties.

That was always Byron.

From the bedroom, the girl's crying turned to full sobs hearing what Byron's was saying in the corridor.

Byron was enjoying it as she realised her fate. Almost as much as Jed's tears.

'This girl Jed,' and he picked up Jed's gun, emptied the cartridge of blanks and put a live one in. 'You know you're right, Jed. They don't pay us enough. You gave me the idea,' he smiled.

The last thing Jed would see.

'I'm gonna be that basking fucking beached walrus—chillin' in the sun when your dust. One sponsor at a time gets me closer and closer,' Byron walked towards the room with the girl in as Jed closed his eyes.

'Now then sweetheart, let's get to it.'

12

THE HADEES ACT

THE FATMAN LIKED to tease. Foreshadowing the lives of his victims. He'd taken to using patsies to test the water with some of the harder targets. He told them what to wear, say; real scripted.

The Fatman was a bit of a writer too.

Mostly, he wanted to test the outcome; the resolve of the targets. A shot across the bows. The Fatman liked to send a testing pain to his victims, before the finishing bolt in an abattoir's pen: sick animals, they didn't stand a chance.

Once there was his guy in Afghanistan: 'You look Malay,' the Fatman had said.

'I'm not.'

'How did you get a job here, with me, looking like that? Don't exactly blend in. Do you? Fuck me. Might as well be Irish.'

'I'm not Malay, or Irish—I told you.'

'Well, just calling it how it is, Bujang.'

'The name's not Bujang either, big man, it's Hadees,' he said.

Vultures circled overhead in a perfectly clear blue sky.

Hadees rolled another body into the ditch like it was a rotting log. The side of the desert track was littered with their victims. Men, women, children and dogs.

'God of War,' the Fatman said and finished cutting a tattoo from the arm of the man in his last breath in the sand at his feet.

A token. A gift to the people who would pay for the man and his family to be erased and end up in the ditch.

In the background a young boy whimpered as he bled out and strained one of his last gasps too, trying breaths through lungs that had been needlessly pierced with skewers from his mother's kitchen.

The Fatman had led a rich Spanish family to believe their daughter had been taken, illegally adopted by the family that used her as a slave. Worse by the father.

The family was now bleeding out in the sand. The Fatman had already been paid by the same family, the ones now dead, to investigate some Italians for a similar wrap.

It was a poetic arc to the Fatman. Putting all parties out of their misery and taking their cash. The men of the households had worked in military units that had some conflict of interest with the Fatman's. Had tread on his toes one too many times. Now he got paid and got rid of the issue.

Both parties had paid up and were taken care of. He still wanted the tattoo. It was symbolic. Much more than it meant to the original bearer. It would form a talking point for the months ahead as he used it as a beer matt.

He held the cut strip of skin up and let the sun bleed through the black and blue inks.

'You're a savage man, sir,' Hadees said.

'And you... You're the God of War, son. Takes one to know one and all that, no?'

'Two e's, sir, not one. It's not Hades. My name, it means...'

The Fatman cut him short: 'Horse shit, son. You're a pure solid gold killer. Just like me,' he looked at the bodies in the ditch. Now, Hadees, with two e's... I've a little acting job that would be right up your street. Looking like that. A Malay and all,' he smiled.

'Eh?'

'Yes, good money too, again,' he folded the piece of skin and put it in the top pocket of his black shirt. The only colour he wore now. To hide the blood-stains. And there were many.

'What're you like at pouring a drink?'

'You want me to be a barman, sir?'

'Yes, and you're welcome, Hadees. With two Es.'

'Where?'

'Oh, you'll love it. Luxury island resort. Topless Western girls. And men eager to tip.'

'They have titties as big as you Fatman? I'm in.'

They both laughed. As the Fatman back-heeled the last body, a young girl, into the ditch and left for a drink. The Fatman had a new beer mat to show off.

13

CHAPMAN'S BAR

'IT WAS LIKE Chapman was never really here: a ghost,' John said to himself as he read a story taped to the countertop of the beach bar. His back was to the waves as his new wife, Cherry, read one of the books she'd found on the island and laid back on a lounger.

A hornbill bird waddled on the end of the bar counter and proudly eyed a bowl of nuts with an air of arrogance as if the island belonged to the wild animals and the birds were lookouts keeping the visitors in check. They were bosses.

The barman busied himself. Pouring, measuring, pouring some more.

'The story of Chapman? Mr Spencer Chapman, sir...?' the Malay-looking man said as he continued mixing an over garnished Virgin Mary. He looked like he knew just fine how the story went, that it was a well-rehearsed feigned curiosity. Complete with a theatrical smirk reflecting in the mirror behind the bar.

John held up a hand so he could see it in the mirror. To stop the barman from putting the vodka in his drink, and as he did, it felt like pulling a broken nail from a toe. Hard as hell but necessary to go on moving. Sobriety was a nagging bitch he hoped would settle down soon. At least for the honeymoon. To give them a chance to bathe and drink down some positive senses, give life a chance, rather than dulling them with the bottle.

John looked across, glancing at Cherry then back down at the laminated story of Spencer Chapman, the bar's namesake, on the bartop. The black and white photos showed an English soldier with a rabble of Malay locals. The text was sun-bleached and unreadable. He had some vague knowledge of Spencer Chapman. The barman filled in the rest, he was well practised and used to telling the story. He obviously waited each time patiently for someone to give him an opening line as John just did.

He was clearly proud to get the tale out with each chance he got. A story for the tourists and visitors. A badge of honour.

'He was a hard Englishman. True soldier. Like us Malays. Like your Norsemen invaders, yes? Vikings.'

'Yes, I guess. They left a lot of themselves behind. In all of us,' John moved one of the readied drinks closer, remembering ghosts he'd seen over the years. He eyed the dark rum behind the counter like it was the last drop of liquid on Earth.'

'Mr Chapman lost all of his team, squad, army-friends. Through disease. Gunfire. Was completely cut off. Escaped the mainland over there,' he waved behind himself, 'in a stolen sub. Yes, very hard-hard man, sir. A Viking.'

John nodded slowly and looked at the clock behind the bar. Time had started to have more importance again. He noticed the seconds passing. Like there was something coming and he wanted them to enjoy what they could, now, before it was too late. Small talk stole these seconds.

The image of the dead orangutan was indelible on their minds and the clock had been ticking ever since.

The bar's own actual clock was fast. Stealing those precious seconds, minutes…pushing at a future he wanted to ignore. He wanted to slow down every moment with Cherry.

The barman turned around again and put his back to John. His words turned grave, sounding like a priest at a dying man's bedside. It was a theatrical piece, it worked: 'Chapman was captured over and over again. By Japanese troops and Chinese bandits. He was tortured and beaten. Still, he stayed strong. The hardest thing that took over him: the jungle. Not a man. The blackwater fever that got to him. It would kill most. He survived it all as well—Viking, yes?'

'Yes.'

'It show's what is possible… if…'

The hornbill on the countertop did a little dance in celebration.

'You've no idea,' John muttered, interrupting. He rubbed a scar on his shoulder, one of many. Then, looked over again at Cherry on the beach.

He'd paused the man's act.

The barman looked disappointed. Lost his flow as he turned back and dropped another drink down and the heavy glass base made a resounding crack, sending the hornbill flying off with a squawk and hurried flap of feathers.

The barman was like a school teacher; slamming a hand on the desk to get John's attention back. He would finish his tale. It's what he did, finish.

He had John's attention back. John stared and another bird landed on the countertop. It was their bar. Their island.

The barman looked unfazed by John's empty black eyes looking through him.

'You see, sir. It goes to show. What one can survive past the un-imaginable. The sheer courage and pain. The mental. The physical. The toughness a body will find, if the spirit within it is hard enough. To endure and to survive.'

John thought of his own Viking inside. A strength of ages, and wondered if that was it. If he'd ever need to call on the darkness to survive again. He'd grown sure of it the past few days. He looked at the bottle behind the bar again and started drinking the rum in his head. He felt it burning the back of his throat. The imagery and sensation were both as real as the Viking's image, a ghost he'd seen over and over in his past. Maybe a visitor and conjured up—he'd forgotten, for now. But the spirit, a hard essence, that would always be there.

John looked at Cherry on the lounger in the distance as the sun arced and the tide turned. He picked up the drinks, smiled a thank you. As his feet left the decking and sank in the scorching sand he thought he heard the barman whisper: 'You were never really here.'

'What?' John said, without turning and closed his eyes a second.

'You're like Chapman. A ghost. Soon to be forgotten.'

He walked on across the hot sand between the palm trees towards the beach, bay and Cherry waiting. She was sat up with books for them both to read.

He opened his eyes, defiant. The seconds ticked and he wanted their time together to be just that; together. And if they were going for a swim they'd do it now before the shark nets were pulled in.

14

HATE TRADER

HE WAS BIG. Overweight. A large man by anyone's standards and a bit of an ox. But, he never sweated. Not as much as people expected anyway. Even when he was jogging, dodging bullets or forcing them down a child's throat. He'd had plenty of moments.

Not a drop. Well, not much.

He'd been through the mill. Secret wars, government-sponsored attacks and under the radar type-shit. Stoking druglords and silencing rebellions one ruthless takedown at a time.

He was morally bankrupt and should have been locked up. He knew early on government sponsorship and backing was a way to exorcise his darker passions. He embraced his carved out career path. Most of all: he loved that ID card that came with the role. Eagles, stars, federal stamps, the whole shebang. Didn't matter what country he was in, it was like waving a dollar around, and the more troubled, struggling and weaker the country he was in the more it opened doors and gained compliance. Fuck, it had even opened a mouth and plenty a pair of legs for him too.

He meant to retire. And he meant to keep that little laminated card and the power it brought.

After everything, nothing made him sweat or fret much. Except 'the sell' he had to do for the benefit of the victims' friends and family when pulling a scam. It didn't come naturally; pretending to care about people's loss. He was getting the practice in, getting better one forced crocodile tear and hand stroke at a time.

He'd found a few memories to dwell back on when he wanted to look as upset as the people he was talking to.

His favourite memory, one he was working at and refining the inner details, was from when he was at school: there was this tank filled with tadpoles in his school class. He loved to sneak in there when no one was looking and flick their little black bodies at the side of the glass so hard their sides split. If they didn't, he had another go until they did.

It was an evolution from his bluebottle game. Where he found hundreds of them by a window box and pulled their wings, lined them up, then splat. One by one until the little wriggling baby fly larvae split out on the window.

When the other children piled into class and saw the tadpole tank with its display of little bodies splattered against the class they'd scream and cry. The Fatman would love it.

Then one day it happened, someone, maybe him, left the curtains open one afternoon by the tank and they all cooked in the sun. The teacher consoled him thinking he was crying and upset at the loss of the mini-class-pets.

It wasn't that which upset him.

He was actually upset he'd lost his play-things. Hundreds of guts he could have split, taken from him. Little grape-like bodies to squash, gone. Taken by the sun.

That memory worked. Summoned half a tear each time.

Then when he needed a little extra help. To look really sympathy laden, and he had to look full cringe-worthily caring:

he'd remember when he'd ripped his piano string on an underage hooker's braces—that never failed to show pain on his face.

He'd never forget the time he recognised this money game either: it was a golden moment. It was way before Jed did, or he'd still be alive. In fact, Jed's last gig was one of the pinnacle moments to start the ball rolling. The Fatman grasped the concept: take people down, then point a finger. Then, get sponsorship from those that missed them for the work already done.

As it was with Jed in the end. God rest his self-righteous dead soul.

He took Jed out, plugged the sorry fuck, and then suggested to the father of the young girl whimpering on the bed in that Artist commune, that Jed had fucked up, got distracted by her tits and then shot his little girl to cover up his indiscretion with the young her.

So, the big man got paid for taking Jed down by the grieving father who was hungry for revenge. Of course, he was. The Fatman had seen to that; that the man craved revenge. The fact of the matter is the Fatman had already taken Jed out, and the little girl down himself. He'd had a little squeeze on those firm young puppies too—before and after they were heaving with fear, then after, when they were slowly calming down, and she was fading out.

He took what he wanted.

Like the tadpoles. The Fatman was a little sad he couldn't have any more fun with the young girl anymore. Still, he imagined tadpoles, bluebottles and hooker's braces on his ripped foreskin every time he needed to summon up a tear.

He already had the photos. Nothing would be broadcast, it was a black ops gig.

The Fatman could take all the money as he pleased from the father, making it seem like he still had a chance to get revenge on Jed. Making it look like he was hard at work. Showing the pics at choice times. Squeezing 'expenses' and final commission outta the father until he had nothing left. How was he to know when looking at the pic of his bloody daughter that Jed's innocent body was behind the camera too already. And that the black angel in front of him was the real killer of both his girl and Jed already.

The victims' family and friends never got to see digital date stamps, all hard copies.

The Fatman loved the tidy synergy. It was a blast.

Like the Irish lads' nail bombing in Birmingham, U.K.. There were victims. Lots of them. And with the lads out the picture, he knew where to point the finger so the victims' friends and family could get some sort of closure, revenge, having seen their loved ones in pieces. John was the perfect patsy. Not least of all because he had some responsibility to bear—like it or not.

It was going to be an easy sell in the hospital grieving room after the bombing: show them the photo of the lad's tattoos, show them John's books with the same titles. Let them join the dots, eyes widen with hate, then, when he could see it in their eyes—pure fucking death stares, then, he'd drop his own bomb: that John should have killed them in the first place. All those years ago. If he'd only filled orders like a good soldier-boy and taken the damn shot.

He must be in on it, right? John? An easy sell. The book names were too much a connection and coincidence. That, and not taking the Irish lads out when he could have. The Fatman couldn't make up a tighter case. For the victims' loved one's to cough up every last note. And to see John burn.

You could trust the Fatman—he'd see to it. Just look at the tears.

He'd let them know alright; he'd get the job done.

This was the Fatman's last outing. A retirement gig. That's why he was drawn to it. It was a bit unusual in that John, the target, hadn't been taken out yet by someone else. But it sure as hell had the perfect setting to start retirement. In Malaysia. And the big man loved those little boys and girls over there. Tight and squealing—how he liked it.

He'd settle the grieving friends and relatives gnawing rage and thirst for revenge for a tidy price. Just covering some modest expenses of course. Flights, drinks, girls, food. A lot of food. Five-star rooms. Taxies. He wasn't fucking walking anywhere, not anymore. Other than to stalk the target. Haunt them both a little. Maybe a little stroll to carve something up they cared about. A lizard, bird or ape.

He'd have to take his squeeze out too, he guessed, Cherry. No biggie.

Bitch had it coming a long time—so the big man had read. As soon as she'd gotten involved with John Black, her card was marked.

The whole situation was sweet. Fact that John was going to be held up at some luxury resort with another load of pricks to get knocked over and robbed made it all the juicier. Easy pickings. It would be the bad-ass big man and an army of pirate-mercs versus a washed-up ex-SAS drunk, John Black, and his new wife, Cherry—RIP. Both weren't tough enough to stay in their vocation. He'd drag them back into his reality.

The big man loved the hard game, fucked it till it split.

He touched it in his pocket: that bit of laminated power. The pant dropper. He fucking loved that little ID card.

THE FATMAN LEANT over on his chair in the Blue Room. Showed them his phone then looked down, in feigned respect, at a threadbare carpet that was as sad and hopeless as these people sat around him.

Tadpoles, think of tadpoles.

'Book covers, who gives a fuck?' said a man in a security guard's outfit. The Fatman assumed he was ex-military. This was gonna be a tough one. He knew the man would wanna get involved and the big American didn't go in for partnerships.

He nodded, thinking: *Tadpoles, splitting, guts hanging. Bluebottles. Splat.*

'Why, Mr whoever… why are you showing us this shit?' the father of one of the dead girls said.

'We thought you were a priest. Come to console us or something, what's this? A game?' an old man quivered looking.

'Thing is. I feel your hurt…' Thinking: *Young girl, black eye. Crying. Teeth brace stuck—cutting into the foreskin. Must cry.*

'I do, I feel it…I've lost people too. Lots of people,' the big man lied.

Ripping her mouth away, bits of foreskin with it.

He lied. The only people he'd lost, he'd taken out himself and then got paid for it.

He started to sweat. Just a bead. This human thing, interacting with words, not brute force wasn't natural to him. Or, trying to appear empathetic.

Tadpoles. Tadpoles. Foreskin. Foreskin.

He just needed to get to the money shot. When they joined the dots and their imaginations ran with him.

The door burst open.

'You're not meant to be in here. Who are you? Out. NOW!' a doctor barked around the doorframe. His eyes were stern as hell. He must have seen more death and suffering than even the Fatman. The doc must have had to make some tough choices. The Fatman knew the look. He'd seen a lot.

An alarm rang out in the corridor and the doctor looked around. 'I've got to go. I want you gone when I get back. Or, with an explanation,' and the doctor left as soon as he arrived. The door shut with a slam.

A light flickered overhead. As sad as the carpet. And the doctor's silhouette moved past the glazed partitioning down the corridor.

The Fatman would have to work hard and fast. Cut to the Chase.

Forcing tadpoles down the young girl with braces' throat—losing them all. No more playthings. Goodnight sweetheart.

A tear nearly came.

Squeezing the dead girl's titties 'till the end. Touching them as they turn cold.

Then it dropped—a single tear. It was all it took to show he might be human to them. Inside he was smiling, counting dollars.

The people in the room were in various stages of grief and looked at the big man with tears on his cheek like he was one of them. And a cure to their pain.

'I'm not your enemy,' he got out another smartphone and brought up more pictures and showed them around. Then he directed his other phone with John's author profile and books around the other way in the circle.

'I don't get it,' the security guard said.

'These lads, boys, ex-IRA bombers… the ones that blew up my little girl, they have tattoos of the titles of this author's books on their arms—what the fuck?'

'Yes,' the big man said and let the facts settle in bed with the lies already laid.

'What the?' the dead girl's father said.

'Seems they were inspired by his words you see,' the big man laid more lies with the truths, 'you see John is connected to them, way deeper than that as well. More than just some abstract mentor...'

'How?' the security guard's teeth gritted down hard. His jaw muscles pushed through his face.

The old man who'd lost his life partner shuffled uncomfortably.

'Those lads you see. Well, you'll have noticed in the papers leading up to the bombing. That they were released onto the streets. Our streets. The papers will join the dots if you don't'

'What about them? What fucking dots?' The girl's father said.

'Well, they got let out, you see. Should have been locked up for good for what they had planned. A bombing. To kill your loved ones. And what do you know, as soon as they're out: bang. They picked right back up where they left off,' and the big man brought his hands together for effect.

Slap.

'What's this got to do with this damn author, J. Black?' the old man said, eyes tightening in.

'He's not just an author. He's an ex-SAS, Ex-gangster. Ex criminal fucker... pardon my language,' the big man feigned respect and used it to draw out the tension, 'and now, yes, an author. Some might say.'

'Fucker,' the security guard clenched his fists with his teeth.

'Cunt,' the grieving old man said. Using the word for the first time in his life.

'Now,' the Fatman took another dramatic pause, reeled them in, 'Now, he's honeymooning on some paradise island in

Malaysia. Prick won't even catch the news of your loss. Too busy swigging cocktails and fucking his new pretty wife...'

'Double-bastard,' the old man said.

'I don't get it?' the dead girl's father said.

'You see, friends,' and the Fatman looked to the floor like he was a consoling priest after all, 'John Black is the reason not only these two bombers got released, re-found their cause, but also that they're still alive to nail bomb this fine city,' he lied again.

The place was a fucking WWII bombed shit hole already as far as the Fatman was concerned. Not to mention the weird-assed accents everywhere. Nothing fine about it at all.

'What the fuck?' the old man said, joining in again, angered to breaking point and impatient to his limits.

'This John Black,' the Fatman started his money shot, 'you see, years ago he was asked to take them out. The lads. To take *the shot* if you like. The government knew what they had planned, and wanted them gone—erased,' this was part truth.

The Fatman had seen John's file. Hell, he was in it himself. The folder was the kind of dirty stuff only his dept ever got to see. Or create. The Fatman had done some extra research. There was enough to hook the victims' interest. 'John didn't do it, see. He pussied out. And these bombers got sent away instead. Got locked up in one of your British criminal training academies. Courtesy of Her Majesty. Meanwhile, after some Witness Protection shit, John progressed up through the criminal ranks of the Manchester underworld. And these lads were studying his form safely inside. Seeing him as an unseen mentor.'

The room nodded along.

'So, when they were released they were back on track. With something to prove to him. To John that is. The same man that saved them. By not taking the shot. That they could live up to *his* standards. Maybe even looking to join his underworld.'

The bullshit was flowing hard out of the Fatman, he'd opened a tap now. He could see they were lapping it up. Bloodthirsty.

'Why are you telling us this?'

'I'm a specialist.'

'What kind of... specialist?' the old man asked.

'Specialising in a certain type of revenge. Hard retribution you might say. Harder than the hate can dish out.'

'I want in. I wanna see this gangster-writer-cunt fry,' the security guard snapped.

'Me too,' the rest echoed.

'Cunt,' the old man whispered. For the last time.

15

UTOPIA FALLS

THEIR WORLD HAD moved, morphing from serenity into chaos in a dance of raging vortexes.

It took less than an hour for the evening's skies to be turned from subtle red hues to pitch black, as the rolling pitches of the sea changed to fierce peaks of crashing waves hosting crazy white horses. Blanketing in a change and a long night of storms shaking the hotel suite. The wooden stilts it stood on creaked a dialogue with the adjoining walkways as they flexed and groaned back at them—bending and twisting in sinister whistling winds. With each crash of waves and flash of lightning, the skies opened up with bright razor cuts that showed a glimpse through to a normally hidden side of life; another universe normally masked from mortal view.

It was a place far away from their idyllic honeymoon island of the day before.

Their personal Utopia, the construct around them and in their heads, was built on dreams. Now, these hopes seemed threatened as the suite's wooden stilts continued to be taunted by the angry waters and under a sky as temperamental as a furious monk about to lose their grip on zen calmness.

The morning brought a new day and a fresh outlook. Leaving the storm's memory in the branches of trees that fell, laying on the walkways and the wooden shutters blown wide.

These memories and clues would form reminders of their moments, so fragile, that would last until another evening of uncertainty.

'Breakfast?' she said from the edge of the bed. Her back arched as if to welcome in the day.

'Breakfast,' he echoed in agreement. Wanting to pull her back into the sheets.

They rushed on with their clothes and walked out. Expecting aftermath. Unsure of what destruction they might see. There was nothing extreme. The island had taken worse and would do again. The clues of the night before were in the leaves, branches and shutters. Almost as if the night was merely a shared dream to contrast the beauty they craved.

A fifteen-minute slow walk to the food hall took them past roosting bats, lounging lizards and more of those thieving troops of monkeys, who eyed them up like teenagers on a rough-arsed council estate.

'You locked the room, right?' she asked, looking at a naughty monkey troop in the treeline.

'Right,' he smiled and threw a nut from the walkway's banister at what looked to be the king monkey that was scratching its arse. The silvered langur grabbed the nut then ate it with one hand and continued preening its head with the other. Taking a flea to its mouth first then the nut.

There was a distinct lack of hornbills en-route. Normally they were everywhere. Black and white flashes overhead and standing guard to the resort's areas.

'Where's our buddies?' she asked. The birds had become their companions on the island and she missed them. Seeing them as unofficial island mascots and guardians.

When they got to the dining hall they realised the birds had beat them to breakfast. Ten or twenty of them were perched, walking and pecking around the food hall tables and counters. Scavenging and looking proud to be there.

'Nasi lemak for breakfast?'

'Nasi lemak for breakfast,' he echoed her.

They'd grown slowly more and more accustomed, then addicted to this rice dish to start their days off. Half sweet, half savoury. Spicy and completely different from what they had at home. Which was rarely anything more than a half mug of half-cold coffee and a slice of toast. Time pressured, he'd grown used to having both in the shower. Now, eating at a table, with Cherry and unpressured seemed as much a break from the norm' as a beach, lounger and pulp paperback.

Time, again, being the most precious commodity.

Local music tinkled in the background, rebounding of marble walls and floors then out through the canvas canopies above. Small groups and individuals went between the different banqueting areas where chefs prepared fresh local dishes and laid them out on platters between giant fruit bowls and exotic dressed drinks.

Alcohol flowed as freely as coffees and teas. Cocktails, champagne, wine and rum. Giant fruit bowls and baskets filled with mangoes, pineapples and melons.

A parrot joined a line of hornbills with a flap of colour to their black and white parade. With it came a different pitched squawk to the ensemble and a flutter of green and yellow feathers.

John sat back on a padded wicker chair and enjoyed the smell from a fresh hot coffee. Time to smell, taste and savour. He closed his eyes and waited for her to return with her drink. The moment carried a breeze that touched him as silk draped over his face.

The seconds slowed as last night's storm faded from view.

The parrot squawked a solo then flew to a nearby palm tree leaving the band of hornbills to it.

A thud of feet went past then another set, heavier than most.

He squinted out the corner of an eye, as a sinister large mass passed by. His eyes snapped open. Then the image was gone. Like a cloud passing in a gust.

He closed his eyes again, frowned, wishing it away. Then he half-opened his eyes again when he heard her sit down opposite. The cups rattled in the saucers.

'I thought I saw... and heard—'

'—the big American...' she finished his sentence. 'From the jungle trek.'

'Yes.'

He'd not gotten irritated by the fact they both seemed to seamlessly finish off each other's thoughts. And echoed each other's thoughts...not just yet. As Cherry finished his sentences—he spoke her thoughts. He imagined it would continue like this for a while; like birdsong, Whilst on the island at least.

Back in England, Manchester or Bristol it just wouldn't work. To twee. Not them at all.

For now, here, they'd play the archetypal love act. Bird song it was. The sweetest music broken by the worry they now shared.

'We don't know it was definitely him... do we?'

'You saw it too then?' John sat up a little to scan the room.

'He might not have done it: that dead orangutan and the clipping in its mouth. Borneo's quite a way away. And there are a few large blokes around here. Look around, it's a help-yourself buffet...we might pile on a few if we keep at it like this,' she patted her waistline like she was ten stone heavier. Or, pregnant.

'He had blood on his hands in that jungle. Literally,' he sat up further to see if he could see the big man.

'How long do we let ourselves try to enjoy this? It is our honeymoon, John,' she pleaded.

John collapsed back into the chair. Heavy with guilt. His mind, his existence—had brought their paths to this. It's who *he* was. Now, it was who *they* were, together.

'I'm not sure how long we can… pretend. I'll try.'

'Let it slide. For now, pet. Just let it go. Please,' she wiped her cheek where a future tear might trail. If he didn't do what she begged.

'I guess you're right,' he knew she always was right, 'or we'll be battling half-truths and paranoias forevermore,' it was their lives back home. He'd tried to write his way out but had just placed them both deeper and deeper in it.

'Who knows, it could be a coincidence,' she shrugged and took a sip. Her cup clanked back into the saucer.

He nodded, buying into the *ignorance is bliss*, she was going for. Right again. They had afforded themselves the ignorance and escape—paid their dues.

'It could be by complete chance that the clipping in the ape's mouth had any connection to you, John. It could have just been a random bit of newspaper to someone, stuffed in a dying animal's mouth,' she seemed to be trying hard. Struggling to convince herself as much as him. 'Who knows, maybe they were trying to help it. Stem the flow. Stop it bleeding out or something. Fuck, maybe it had eaten it itself. There's plenty of rubbish on those trails.'

He nodded, 'I'll try and leave it alone. If you can. I will. Promise,' and he took a drink.

'I already have,' she looked unconvinced.

They were married now. This is what he understood
happened in marriages. Anything to protect the other half. Their
feelings. Absolutely anything.

'I'm going for a refill. You want some?' she asked, smiled and
stood up with both their cups already in her hands. She knew he
did.

THE BREAKING CHINA stopped the room dead, the music,
the chatting—the birds all froze still. Everything connected. The
Idyllic surrounds, setting and room were sliced open like the
night skies canvas in the previous night's storm. In a temporal
flash of disturbance to shatter and destroy it all.

Alongside the coffee station was a long table. Usually
full of papers for every nationality, this time it was aimed at
them: full of Brit' tabloids and broadsheets.

All the headlines told the same story:

IRA DENIES BIRMINGHAM BOMB BLAST

–

STILL PICKING UP THE PIECES
17 DEAD. 22 INJURED
(SO FAR)

–

BOYS RELEASED. TO KILL AGAIN

–

REOPENED CITY CENTRE DESTROYED.
BULLRING WEEPS

–

She apologised to one of the waiters for dropping the coffee
cups to one of the waiters who nodded meekly and busied

himself in tidying. Another had rushed over to check she was alright.

She smiled apologetically and walked back to John and their table without coffees.

He stood up slowly as she was walking over. He looked as if he was about to rush to her and had changed his mind; visibly worried she might be hurt or scared— but then noticed that look in her eyes protecting him instead. It was something else she'd shown him before in those eyes and written across her face: a warrior's rage. Protector. Lover.

She stood in front of the table where he sat and nearly told him not to move. Not to go over to the table where she'd been. That there was no point in reading the headlines. There was only one that mattered, their own:

Utopia had fallen.

16

A NIGHT TO REMEMBER

THEY HELD EACH other, trying to sleep. Trying to forget.

Another storm outside. White noise to a worse one raging up in their heads. They had an urge to arm themselves in the morning. Confront the island. Push back at the reality disintegrating around them.

Maybe they were all in on it? Everyone else on the island.

Then the thoughts would subside, for a while. Like the waves outside. Letting them grab moments of hope. Respite.

Another coincidence. The connection between emotions and weather.

But the thoughts never changed enough that they could lower their guards and drift into a restful sleep fully.

The realisation was always there. Even if no one was taking ownership of the provocations aimed at John, them both. Maybe they just wanted to get into their heads.

It had already happened.

The boys had been released. John's moralistic choice of his past, in not killing them, had led the boys into doing what they longed to anyway. To destroy. Nothing had changed other than his and their destinies were to be forever interwoven in an ugly tapestry of blood and hate.

'Tomorrow, we go off-grid.'

'I thought we already had,' she rolled over and stroked his face, 'aren't we too late for that?'

He sat up and looked at the mini-bar humming in the corner.

'I'm not sure that's going to help.'

'I was thinking of you,' he partially lied. Wanting a drink more than ever.

SHE PURRED, FAST asleep. It was the most beautiful thing he'd ever heard. Until she started talking in her sleep as well. The words were unmistakably worried, troubled... he clenched his fists. Eyes squeezing shut.

He wished he was someone else, for her.

He thought her purring was echoing at first. Then a noise grew louder, like a mosquito that was battling the curtains and windows. It faded in and out. Then another joined in.

He sat up slowly and quietly, not wanting to disturb her sleep, and padded through to the bathroom.

He looked in the large circular mirror above the sink. A porthole to a man he never thought would see the age he had become, let alone be married.

The buzzing noises vibrated around his head. He shook once, twice, tightly closing his eyes shut then opened them again.

The image. A ghost had returned.

He froze. He hadn't seen the Viking in a long time. Never this close. And never without a tanker full of drink to blame the apparition on. He touched the mirror and the Viking looked to his left. John followed the warriors gaze out of the open sides to the bathroom, out to sea, into the distance over the black waters.

He squinted at shapes in the distance.

The noises, the vibrating and buzzing was coming from them; black shapes on the horizon. Small boats with outboard motors drifting. Observing. Waiting for something.

His bare feet on the wooden boards felt cold for the first time since he could remember. The hairs on his arms and neck stood up. His scars itched and his tattoos burned. He stepped towards the infinity bath—filled, its water black, like the sea and moonlit blood.

The hotel suite rooms started to move, like they were all afloat. He looked through the open walls of the bathroom to the night sky as the clouds parted long enough for him to see the plough: Karlavagnen. Or, The Chariot of Man.

He looked back at the mirror. The Viking's arm slowly outstretched from it. Then, came a finger, which drew lines in the air, making three interlocked triangles—the sign for Valhalla:

John fell to his knees as if to pray.

Outside, the boat motors revved hard, in unison, then stopped.

He rocked backwards then forwards in a trance. Then rolled sideways into the bath. The black blood swallowed him whole and he disappeared under the thick fluid, like oil.

17

PIRATES

KNOCK. KNOCK.

'It's room service.'

He woke. Startled at the noises in the room rather than his head for a change. Confused. Battling the night before: a dream, nightmare, whatever the darkness had brought. He touched his arm which was wet and then the bed which was soaked through where he'd laid. Sweat, water, blood—he wasn't awake enough to separate the three from illusion and reality.

Had he drunk? Or was it just for her?

KNOCK. KNOCK. The beats were more instant this time. Demanding attention.

'Room service…'

She was startled with him this time opening wide too. Appearing delayed by the previous night's drinks. Her eyes looked reluctant to see the day. Awake. She looked at John. Then looked scared.

'Did we order anything?'

'No,' he said.

'You look more troubled than yesterday. Get much sleep?'

'I thought I saw something last night…'

'What?'

'I dunno,' he looked at the door where the knocking was coming from. 'It could have been a dream.' He touched the wet bed sheets again, uncertain of his own senses. The World about him. Was any of it for real?

He touched a scar on his shoulder from a bullet he'd taken for her. Then the burn marks on his forearms. Burned for not firing at the teenage boys in Ireland. These were real.

'Miss, sir… we need to talk. Open up,' came the voice from the other side of the door. And repeated knocks of a fist. Or something harder—like metal.

'What was it? What did you see?' she said and joined him looking to the door as it rattled with each knock.

He stood and moved towards the door… so disorientated, dizzy. Feeling intoxicated and she was the one who drank the half bottle of Jack D last night. Right? Not him.

'I saw some boats on the horizon. Drifting. Like they were watching the island. Preparing for something. Watching. Waiting.'

'A dream?'

'Yes. I don't know anymore, what it was… and isn't,' he reached for the key, hesitated, turned it and then opened the door ajar. Head spinning.

'Maybe they've come to tell us something, to take us away from the Thai side of the island. The storms *are* getting worse?'

'Pirates,' he said.

'What?'

A rifle butt came through the doorway and into the bridge of John's nose.

He passed out.

He faded away, again, as last night and the days either side joined, merged and blended like a Mobius strip. All joined. No beginning, No end.

His last thoughts before passing out, filled with anger at his own stupidity. Thinking: always… always go with the gut.

Their denial had lasted until breaking point. Chasing a dream they thought they deserved, for one short break, at least.

Now he was broken. And she screamed in the background. The honeymoon turned blood-bath.

Fade out.

From the blackness the Viking resurfaced. Battle. Blood. Death to follow.

18

CAGED ANIMAL

THE BIG AMERICAN pissed down from up high. His stinking foetid urine splattered the bars of John's bamboo cage and the leaves and dead insects on the floor. He hadn't drunk as much as he should have given the climate and the dark concentrated flow was like a pungent treacle. Sticky, stinking and unavoidable.

He aimed his cock, fat, like the rest of his body, with one hand and filmed the degradation on one of his mobiles with the other. He was a good shot with both. He'd done this before. He was the master director of his own underground series. Coming soon to the one seat cinema in his head.

'Looks like I haven't been drinking enough water, John.

A nearby parrot squawked as leaves fell and rested on the cage's bars.

'Been a busy bee haven't I. Lots to do. Lots—and lots—to do. Best to keep hydrated though isn't it though, John. And you never know when I might need to take another piss.'

He shook off and kicked the bars. Lit up a smoke and flicked the still-burning match down at John. The flame was extinguished by the steaming wet urine all around the cage.

John half opened an eye caked shut with dried blood from his nose and stinging from the

piss.

'I might have some of that durian fruit. Potent. Rank. Dunno why they eat that shit. These fuckers? Broccoli makes my piss stink like shit too… it's gonna make it real nice for you, John. That's a great idea for the next round isn't it, John?'

John looked up, his eyes looking crazed, in a place between worlds. The

Fatman had crushed his reality. Brought his past back and used them to crush John's hopes and a future. All had merged. Just how he'd planned.

'Where is she?' he muttered.

The Fatman ignored it.

The big man meant to break him. To exploit the image of it. He knew what buttons to press; child's play, he'd done that all before too. By coincidence…with children. The big man had no moral compass and he resented John for what he'd read of his.

He had fucked up the Fatman's plans in the past. No more.

Take the shot, John.

In fact, John was so tightly woven into this plan. His moral misjudgement had initiated, crafted and formed the end piece perfectly. A master craftsman. Hell, if he didn't know any better the Fatman would have thought John had planned all out himself.

'Just a little video for our sponsors back in the U.K. Johnny-son,' the big man waved the mobile around pointing the camera through the bars to capture the look on John's face, or lack of it, and the piss steaming from his body and the dank bamboo cage he was in.

There wasn't enough blood or reaction. The Fatman was a director of hurt. And the picture wasn't quite right yet.

The Fatman grabbed a bamboo pole, leftover from crafting the cage, and jabbed at John like he was stoking a fire to life.

'Bleed, fucker, bleed.'

A giant fat centipede crawled over John's arm. He looked too subdued, in another place, to notice or flinch.

'Perfect,' the Fatman chuckled. 'So sweet,' he shook his head in disbelief at how well it was going now.

The fire stoked.

John's unblinking eyes looked up through the dim light as the big man's piss dried over his face and the flash on the phone camera strobed and flashed through the bars again.

'Must sting that, eh, John?' the Fatman stopped sniggering and shifted gear to a serious tone.

John looked as though he tried to respond. Nothing. His chin moving up, lips trying to part. Emptiness coming out.

'Really must sting, don't it, John, that all those bomb victims' friends and family despise and hate you so much. And that *they'd* pay to see you suffer like this.'

John's face winced.

'That's right, John. They paid for this. All of it.'

John shook his head slowly.

'It's if you made the fucking nail bomb yourself... Well, that's the idea I gave them,' he laughed. Pleased with his work.

John clenched his hands in the dirt.

'The idea was an easy one to sow. To get them to believe you played the key part. Shit, John. You did anyhow. Whether you grasp it or not. You really should have taken those shots back in Ireland all those years ago, John. Shouldn't you?'

John's eyes opened a little as if he started to recognise the Fatman a little. Then he closed them and seemed to fade away back into his nightmare.

'Couldn't just do as you were told though could you, John? Couldn't just follow the orders, and take those little Paddy pricks down?'

The centipede was back. And a cockroach too.

'Doesn't matter, now, all you did was give them time to lose their conscience even further whilst locked up inside. Bitter seeds sowed.'

The cage creaked and the jungle around them joined in. Noises, animals, waiting for scraps.

'They fucking loved your books inside, John.'

John visibly strained to sit up as much as he could, putting his hands around the bamboo bars to form tight fists.

'Strange how everyone and everything is so connected, isn't it, John? We're all on the same journey. Things pre-decided. You can't escape it, John. The lads couldn't. You can't. She... can't.'

A crack of lightning overhead signalled another heavy pour to come. A day of degradation had passed. The storms had grown more and more sure to come at night.

The sounds of waves would usually massage the island's newly-weds and other visitors to sleep as the rains freshened up the life on the island for a new day in the evening. Now, the mood has changed. Nature's sounds tried to cover the sounds of the screams, gun cracks, shouts and yells that filled the island as the pirates had their way.

'Did you really think you'd just marry up, settle down and hide from it, John? Your fate was decided when you didn't carry out that fucking order—to shoot those Irish boys, John.'

Another gunshot in the background. Neither the Fatman nor John jumped at it.

Ghosts stirred.

'Your fate was even more decided as it was MY FUCKING ORDER, John,' his teeth gritted.

John's eyes changed and the American could see a mental coin drop behind them. He covered his mouth with a cupped hand and repeated the words from all those years ago as a reminder: 'Greenlight. Cleared. Take them down. Go. Go. Take them out, John. Now. Fire. What are you waiting for? Take the fucking shot, John. NOW!'

John glared.

'Ring any bells, John?' he knew it did.

John started to shake uncontrollably.

'You see: those marked for death, the lads, needed to be dissolved—it was their fate. And that order you ignored... well, some rich fucks paid me a lot of money to persuade you and your lot to let me—give you—that command.

More screams. Shots.

'There's always a bigger picture, John,' the Fatman looked around, opened his palms and took ownership of the sounds of the island. The sounds of pain.

John's eyes looked as though they were getting noticeably blacker with each second.

'The same rich fucks that paid for me to get you to take that shot... they wanted me to make sure the lads blew themselves up when they got out... and that you suffered soon after. Like now. And what d'ya know. I'm only gonna get paid all over again by those same fucks. Then there's the victims' family and friends coughing up to see you burn: sweet. Then, all these rich cunts you're holidaying here with here too: the island safes are an easy pick. And then... then, comes the really good bit,' he knelt, looked down deep into the cage, smiling. 'Then... there's the money I get for your lady.'

John looked like a statue in black stone. Frozen over at the sound of the Fatman's voice. Like a statue. A robot. No longer looking human at all.

'Yes, John, the underworld skin-trade here pays well to fuck a western ex-copper. Over and over. They'll keep her going for months. Until they get bored and the rot sets in, of course.'

A group of bats flew over undeterred by the gunfire and flames.

'Don't worry I'll get my piece of her first, John.'

The Fatman threw his spent cigarette into the cage. 'Dirty fucking habit. Remember why I gave up now,' the Fatman sneered.

John seemed to grow slightly, nearing the slides of the cage.

'Nearly over for your part in this. Took a while but we got there in the end, didn't we, John? Now, let's take it to a vote from our sponsors. Let's hear what they want doing with you,' he stood back up, pressed the mobile's screen and raised it to his ear.

JOHN COULD HEAR his pulse in his ears.

Bang. Bang. Bang.

His tinnitus has returned echoing gunshots of his past and with those on the island. It came back with images of ghosts he'd thought he'd long since said his goodbyes to.

The first time he saw the Viking was back in Ireland when he didn't take that shot. Now he was back. Fierce as hell.

Pirates might bleed the island into the sunset. But, a Viking was eager to bring hell-fire with dawn.

The warrior's image merged in and out of John's head. Their heritage, past and present as co-joined as ever. As much as what he needed to do.

John shook like he was in ice water as body and mind fluxed, morphed and convulsed.

The adrenaline and situation were birthing new demons.

The big American might have thought it was by his design. But it was John who would unleash this ancient warrior from his own cage.

He wanted a drink more than ever.

His buried voices were back. Bloody tendencies returned.

They'd never *really* left.

The Fatman grinned down at him like a viper. Listing out options he'd put to a vote over the phone. Ways to best dispose of John, make him suffer for the victims' appeasement at the loss of their loved ones.

'A slow cage drowning seems popular. Are we going with that?' He paused as the people on the other end of the line must have been deliberating.

John only heard a few words next: 'sharks, cut, ditched'.

Then came the rifle butts through the bars.

He tried to cover his arms and face but the cage was too tight a space. And he shook hard. He couldn't stop. Each strike beat him further into his full darkened transformation.

A knife through the bars.

A cut to a forearm. A leg.

Black. Thick blood.

THEY DITCHED HIM in the cage over the side of a boat. Weighed it down like a giant lobster trap and filmed it slowly sinking. His eyes faded in and out of consciousness as they pointed the phone over the side.

The last image of the Fatman came as he leaned out the side of the boat, looked to say something into the phone, pointed one last time then waved and grinned.

The cage sank away into an azure blue that gradually faded to black.

Like oil.

Like the bath John had fallen into in their room.

Hell-fire comes on a new dawn.

19

VIKING

THE SALTWATER STUNG the cuts on his face and woke him. The blackness faded back to the azure blue backlit by a full moon. Beautiful hues from the surface of the water's surface seen for the seabed shimmered, reflecting up, down and through the currents.

The Fatman's desire for theatre was a mistake—they should have just killed him.

He'd been reborn from harder waters than this before.

The boat had left, sure of his death, as he lay on the seabed by the cracked open cage that had split on one of the rocks they'd weighed it down with.

A cage of hollow bamboo trunks, filled with air.

He convulsed, kicked and lashed outs—he'd had a fit—convulsions. Broke the cage. The moon, situation and lightning from underwater had all born a monster.

The cage was balsa wood to him. The island: dust.

He didn't feel the need to breathe. Was he dead? Or had all those times she'd stopped him smoking and drinking finally paid off? And he was actually alive more than ever?

His heart beat hard in his ears. *Thump. Thump.* As if he was the waves: he was alive.

A push with strength for her he moved up.

Slowly surfacing, his eyes peered above the waterline, as he looked back at the once tranquil island resort, now lit up by the moon and fires. So many fires.

A war zone. His domain.

Towers of smoke spiralled up from different areas as occasional cracks of gunfire echoed accompanied by screams. The island won, the pirates still rampaged into the night.

A hairy wild boar swam past and looked at John with human-like eyes. Knowing. Empathy. Fear.

The island had become frantic and the animals were fleeing the flames and gunfire. Now John was back, there was something else too—to flee from.

John blinked as the last of the blood from his eyebrows crossed his eyes. The saltwater sealed his wounds.

His life was predestined to violence, he knew that now and wanted a drink.

He should never have involved Cherry in any of it. That's what love is. To bury self-interest and keep them away when it's best for them.

The Fatman and pirates had started a war. Now John swam at it willingly. Smiling with the Viking inside of him. He longed to burn them all. And for him: to be welcomed into Valhalla.

His blood must have attracted sharks, and that's what they wanted; the Fatman and his sponsors. He moved fast through the water. Covered by night. The fish stayed at bay. Easier fresher prey to catch.

He crept up the shore, dripping as he walked past more wild boar going the other way, escaping their homes.

He knelt under the wooden stilts of their once tranquil honeymoon suite which what seemed a few hours previous had been the epicentre of joy. In ignorance of the truth now confronting them. Now, it would be a space to re-calibrate and welcome in the darkness.

Why had he answered the door?

Why had they stayed on the island after reading the headlines?

As he walked up the beach the questions kept coming. Hindsight was a bitch of a taskmaster. He knew the answers.

The contents of one of the room's mini-bars were scattered in sharp grasses at the edge of the beach. He grabbed a bottle of dark rum like it was a snake to throttle. And then a half bottle of Jack Daniels.

He remembered giving the first half to her to drink the night before. To rest up and forget their worries. Now, it was too late. They'd come head-on. Here it was, what was left of the bottle—his tonic.

He couldn't remember his own last drink. Manchester. Bristol Maybe. He didn't need to. He was going back inside himself—resetting to a bad side. All those times and places. Gangs and wars. Loves and hates.

The drink would be the elixir; coating the knife he'd cut them with.

Untethered, again. *Transferred* back into the darkness and *divided* from those he loved: Cherry.

The *Viking* was back.

As a new day dawned, the jungles of the island turned black.

He drank the Jack D bottle down and crept along the raised wooden walkway back to his and Cherry's suite on stilts over the beach and sea. He put the rum bottle carefully down by the door but held onto the Jack bottle tight by its neck. Hesitant, in case anyone was still inside their suite.

He put an ear to the door as a rustling and a knock came. Someone was still searching inside.

John smiled. Elated. Thirsting for a kill.

He tapped gently on the door, 'room service,' ironically echoing the words that had spiralled them down into this place and time.

His comedy high pitched voice stopped the person inside.

The door opened as if arrogantly not expecting any risk.

There was risk. More than sharks in the sea.

The man who answered didn't get a chance. His nose was weaker than the base of the Jack D bottle which stayed intact. It was still in one piece when it crushed the man's eye socket. And...when the door closed behind John and the man's face was battered into a concave Eton mess on the floor.

The fire raged in the blackness of John's eyes.

John slowly reopened the door, casually picked up the rum bottle from outside and closed it again. He unscrewed the bottle and took another deep swig. He eyed the pirate on the floor like a wounded insect and gauged whether the mercenaries black fatigues would fit him.

The body coughed up blood in gasp. Still alive.

John ignored it and yanked the pirate around like a dummy. Undressed it then piled it into the bathtub which re-coloured to deepest crimson. Blood like oil.

John redressed. For war.

The body started to gasp and blew a blood bubble as a face looked out from the surface of the bathwater. The man was still alive, barely. John reached over, buttoning up the pirate's black shirt he now wore, leaned over and pushed the man's face under. The body started to shake, splashing in protest, fighting for life.

John knelt and whispered to the water's surface as it slowly stilled: 'You're the lucky one, first out, less suffering that way...'
He stood and looked out at the moon, drank the rum and looked

around for a smoke. Surely the pirate had some? It came with the job, didn't it?

John's notebook lay on the floor discarded by the pirates. Meaningless to them.

He bent down, picked the Moleskine up and put the man's pistol that had been casually laid on the bed, in the back of his belt and pocketed the ammo clips. Then, he inspected the AK-47 with a cut down stock that leant by the cupboards. John looked for damage; jamming or anything that would taint his new relationship with it.

'This is marriage,' he said and kissed the side of the automatic rifle. 'Til death do us part.'

The waves crashed outside as the struggling sunrise was covered by clouds. John kept drinking and listened to the dead man's walkie talkie on the bed. He wanted to build a mental picture of how many there were out there. How savage they were, who the leader was. Beyond the Fatman. And most of all, what they'd done with Cherry.

HE DIDN'T UNDERSTAND Malay, but he got the general gist. They spoke in a bastardised mix of languages with Malay at the base. He recognised the words: red-haired bitch, for Cherry. And, writer-cunt, for him. Undoubtedly started by the Fatman.

The pirates had spread out around the island. Had arrived in two offences, which is why John and Cherry were caught off guard by the knock on the door, and the rifle butt to the face. That and their general confusion and their lives having gone haywire so quickly.

As John'd been watching the boats on the horizon outside. Another landing party must have already hit the other side of the island, taking Chapman's bar and the bay it fronted onto.

It sounded like the key island resort hot spots had been turned into mini bases and camps; a few men at Chapman's Bar, a mini battalion at the cliffs and another by the foodhall and main jetty.

He wanted to kill them all.

To get to her.

20

THE JUNGLE TURNED BLACK

HATAR LOOKED AT his own body in disbelief. Starting with the right hand that held the handgun he pointed at the quivering Westerners under a palm tree. Then he glimpsed at his wrist, turning it as if he held a heavy stone. His eyes then moved up his arm past a series of barely healed scars. Like folded crushed leaves pressed into his skin. Permanent marks left from the board he was made to run into on his training day. Pulled aside a moment early from death a moment too late to save his flesh all together.

They'd pulled him aside, the senior pirates, mere milliseconds to spare.

It seemed a random choice. One that was yet to show any personal reward to Hatar. He didn't even know if his family had been receiving the dollars he'd set aside. The pirate leaders asked all the recruits how much they wanted to send. And docked it from pay they never actually saw themselves. It was the last chance, bottom of the barrel, putting faith and trust in the untrustworthy.

Through sheer desperation—he'd put what was left of his faith in pirates—it had come to that.

Hatar struggled to believe what had happened to his and his family's life. Those things that had gotten so desperate, so as to take the ultimate plea: to put that trust in killers and thieves.

What's more: to become one himself.

Disbelief.

The friend he'd joined with hadn't been so fortunate. Running headlong into the glass spikes on the board.

Maybe he was the lucky one?

Did his friend get to escape?

Was he trapped in some sort of nightmare?

Why was he now inflicting this pain and worry onto others? These random, rich Westerners? So random. So rich. Poor dogs. Then he thought: *rich. There's the answer. The reason why.*

The small group of white scared faces under the palm tree could afford to worry. To travel around the world in shiny shoes and brand new outfits. Knowing they could escape afterwards onto a plane. Antietam they liked. To be gone. Rest their heads on soft beds made of silk, Egyptian cotton and dream the dreams of the privileged. They might as well have been royalty.

That's why he did it...

Hatar could afford none of it and would cut off his left nut for a fraction of what they had. As it happens, there was an easier way. To take by force. And he had to do. For the money. So his boys, sick wife, could eat—not much at that: rice bowls and fish scraps at best.

He had to have faith. Ignorance is bliss. Tell himself whatever he needed to get by— just like everyone else. A story to be told. The scared Westerners cowering under the tree were probably telling themselves one right now, a story: that this was all just a bad dream, everything was going to be okay. Any time soon they'd wake up. Or, a hero would save them.

Hog Shit.

There were no heroes here. Only pain. Barbarity. And people like Hatar that had sold their soul to dish it out.

He parked the moral quandary and returned to his rage—his own escape. Aiming it at those that seemed gifted from up on high into riches he could never imagine. He walked over to the palm tree and hit a woman square in the face with the butt of his handgun. She was about the same age as his wife and hadn't missed a meal in her life. His own wife was lucky to see a meal every few days. Or, his boys. He missed them most of all.

Then he swiped the man with the butt of his gun again and again. Obviously, the woman's new husband as he'd protested at his wife getting hit. It was definitely his turn. A parallel version of himself—he hated him most of all.

They whimpered. Cried. Sobbed. All of them.

Just noises to Hatar. Nagging in his ears. Bleating sheep waiting to be slit from ear to ear. His conscience stepped in again, for a moment: the man could actually be him. So, he smacked him again and the morality disappeared with a splash of red to the tree trunk. As the man's blood hit the tree bark the woman's tears hit the sand and the waves crashed beautifully in the background.

A picture postcard luxury retreat. Poetry in motion, blow after blow.

The whips of his hands dished out this bleak prose in tune with nature. Of course, it was on his side: the island. Harbourer of beasts.

The Westerner's blood dried quickly on the sand and trees. It'd been a hot day and the beach absorbed and scorched it like an oven. Storing it up like his bottled emotions. Ready to fry whatever touched it.

Pigs, he thought. *Gluttonous pigs* who don't know how lucky they are to roll in the shit gifted to them. *Greedy, rich pigs*—and that's the story he'd tell *himself* to get by. So that he could believe his boys and wife could eat from the dollars he sent.

He despised the tourists as they cowered under the tree. He hated them because they stood out against the idyllic background they were holidaying in. All of them shining beacons to what he'd become. Death and despair.

He shook his head, knelt down and took a swig of water from the pink bottle at the woman's feet. She wept uncontrollably.

As he stood he felt a sudden pressure about his neck, his head forced to one side—then there was a look in their eyes, those faces at the base of the tree: they'd seen something, someone they feared more than him... And it had him by the head and neck.

A snap in his spine. More pressure from behind. Crack.

An image came of his family laying starving on the floor of their crowded slum hut. Not having received a single dollar. He couldn't save them. It was all in vain.

Then, the point of his own blade protruded from his chest. Forced through from the back Taken from its sheath by a ghost. A demon he never saw coming. One much worse than which he'd become.

THE BARMAN ON the other side of the island grinned. The Fatman had it planned out all right, perfect. This was such easy picking. An island full of rich fucks to rob and this shamed writer-man to be humiliated and get paid for it. Even more easy money.

Kerching.

Even better, he got to stand watch at the island's well-stocked Chapman's Bar.

He poured himself a messy tequila sunrise with crushed ice and watched one of his comrades pushing a girl around. Her partner lay bleeding on the floor from a head wound, maybe dead, maybe not. Probably soon would be if no one did anything. And no one was going to.

The sorry, fuck.

The couple's honeymooning resort had obviously turned black for them, like the jungles of all about them. The pirates had cut the lines and secured the reception room first of all. Where everyone kept their phones. The mobiles alone would fetch a tidy sum along with everything else in the safe.

Such fat wealthy bastards—he hated them all.

'He's still moving,' he said looking at the man on the floor, slowly moving an arm feebly.

The barman's pal was busy pulling at a girl's shirt to expose her breasts… and resented any interruptions. Savouring new flesh. He quickly ran over and hit the wounded man with his rifle butt.

'Not anymore he isn't…'

The man returned to his prize; her voice caught short, in shock at the loss of her new husband. Breasts heaving. Wet and wide puppy dog eyes, sadder than a dying orphan.

The barman had no commitments anymore outside of his work. That is why the Fatman took to him. Similar priorities: one last bang and bust job—then on to retirement. That's what he told him.

He quite fancied the Fatman in a way. But kept that to himself. Unsure if the Fatman liked men, girls, boys or women. Sometimes he wondered if they were both the same person. Genes parted at birth and grown-up on either side of the World. Essentially, they were the same being in his eyes, despite his brash American ways. And he, the barman, much more considered and thoughtful.

They could be together. He pondered.

Maybe when all this was done with, their genes would resplice. Join back together. They would be happy. Talking and joking about the young heads they'd robbed, bashed and fucked.

That was the barman's story, for now, the one he dwelled on, that got *him* by.

A gunshot from the treeline sent a flock of birds flying.

He took a sip of his triple strength cocktail and ignored it. There were plenty of shots ringing out as the Pirates had taken over and were having their fun.

They owned the island now, the Pirates. Even the animals were fleeing.

Bang. Another shot.

He looked up to see the girl with her breasts out. Confused. She was now covered in someone else's brain and blood. Bits of skull hung from her dusty blonde hair. His fellow Pirate was alongside her on the floor, legs twitching, his head was an angry mess like a bag of smashed crabs.

The barman ducked behind the counter.

He looked for his gun and peered through the bamboo slats to the front and side of the bar's counter. His eyes darted. Hunter, now the hunted.

What was out there?

Normally, he was more focused than this. A warrior. Something in this situation had him spooked. Like the universe had seen his mind's eye, seen him fantasising about the Fatman and him together. Repulsed at the notion and had decided to put an end to it… and him.

The tourist-honeymoon girl lay curled into a foetal position and tried to cry the situation away but she'd no more left in her. Dry pain.

A lone bird called as if a starting signal.

But, for what?

Then, the singing started, quiet at first. Coming from the jungle. A drunken Western man's voice:

Eyes... I've eyes only for you.
My darling.
Deepest browns to black.
Are we in heaven or hell?
Only, my love.
These eyes... for... you.

The barman shuffled uncomfortably. Pains in his thigh from the floor matching those in his ears from a madman's chants.

Hands... my sorry hands for you.
A writer's digits... now with arms.
About your throat.
Hands—FOR YOU.

The barman looked around panicking. The song moved all around in the wind. A haunting chant that scratched at his eardrums and hurt deep inside: needles, heartburn and acid.

'What do you have for me?' a voice whispered from behind the bar.

He jumped and the bird called again.

The barman's body jolted. He spotted his rifle under the clothes and bar rags where he'd dropped it earlier. He reached over. He hadn't needed to use it yet.

It was too late. He would get a chance to.

A wild animal... a black mass, launched over the countertop onto him. A boar, an angry rabid monkey... something else. Stiff and heavy, like a wet tarpaulin.

It sang and spat at him:

TEETH.

I only have teeth—for you.

It dripped blood and spat into the barman's mouth and eyes. The mass pinned him down. And battered him, bit at him. Feral. Bottles, fists. Bits of cheek and nose gone. He felt what was left go with a crackdown to his core, then those cheekbones smashed. Then forehead. He feared his brain was already on the sand being pecked at by birds.

It was.

He imagined the Fatman one last time. In what was left of his head he saw it: drifting past pain to death. The Fatman laughed at him. The way he did—a beautiful walrus. Divorced from humanity. He told him he'd no chance—he wasn't his type.

The barman cried a final tear...fearing he was alone for death.

Then, he saw a Viking, with a fist about to smash through his skull. Into the sand underneath him. Then grabbing his heart as it still beat and devouring it like an overripe stinking durian fruit.

FIVE PIRATES LOOKED over the mini-cliff at the bodies they'd been throwing over to the pit below, casually and experienced as if they were fly-tipping rubbish bags. They'd taken watches, wallets, necklaces and rings, all laying in a heap behind them.

One of the group pointed. 'Look, that one... still moves. Still alive.'

Another unzipped and started to piss a giant arc onto the twitching man who lay on top of the pile of bodies below.

'Die you fuckers,' one of them said.

They'd saved bullets. Their rifles were laid up against a tree behind them. The same tree they'd swung the Westerners at, with arms tied behind their backs. The Pirates went about killing them on the cheap, held them by their feet and swung them at a nearby trunk: Khmer Rouge style. If they swung hard enough the head's damn near came off. It became a bit of a game. Tiring as much as it was fun. But it was fun to them.

Now, they looked over the edge and rested.

'You think these lot thought they could buy happiness over here?'

'Should have stayed home,' one of them replied

'YOU should have stayed home,' came a voice from behind them in the trees.

The AK47 is an easily maintained toy gun to some. But it kills. Rarely jams without easy release: pop, pop, pop.

One by one they knelt down. Knees shot out from the back as a spray of bone and blood slashed out over towards the bodies in the pit.

Pop. Pop. Pop.

In pain. And shock. Knees and shins in tatters. Splintered.

Something much darker than their actions swept over the part of the jungle they were in.

THEY CHOKED ON the gold. The rings, The watches and even the wallets. He made sure of it.

Their own bullets were spared again. As they bled out slowly and choked on the Westerners' jewellery. Blood splattering dead leaves all around them. As he forced the metal down their throats.

JOHN WATCHED FROM the shadows of the trees like a hungry wolf on an island that was full of lambs. His history, training, experience and desire was nothing in comparison to the savage ghost that now dominated his every being.

Having dispensed with those in his way, he was continuing on his way to Cherry. Anything and everything in his sights was prey.

SINBAD SANG TO himself. He wasn't sure where the song had come from, maybe the Tannoy before they cut the wires, or from the radio in the car to the jetty.

Maybe, one of the other Pirates had been singing it over their radios as they went about their killing spree—*yes*.

It had stuck anyway, 'Eyes for you… only my eyes for you,' he sang like a crazily happy mad man. And Sinbad was. Crazy, and happy. Waiting to unwrap his present. The woman he watched over, Cherry. She had a blindfold on and thick industrial tape around her hands behind her back on the chair. If he'd found a bow, it would have been put on her head.

Sinbad didn't know her true value.

The big American Fatman had made it clear: do nothing, until he gave the word… But, not to worry. When he *did* say the word—then, it would be an eat as much as you can buffet. To go wild. Fuck the bitch up. Feast. Devour her all up.

And that's why Sinbad sang. Happy in anticipation. More than the money coming, he loved to fuck. Invited or not. Most of all: Western, rich bitches.

He wandered away from the chair she was on. Strolling casually, like taking a meandering amble whilst always having an eye on the prize. In the background of the food hall, a few other Pirates milled around. Kicking a tourist here, spitting out some gourmet chunks of over prepared food over there.

Sinbad was in heaven. His own luxury island resort. He couldn't have designed it easier himself.

He walked back over to Cherry, 'I couldn't have designed this better myself, lady,' he lifted her blindfold, revealing hate-filled and bloodshot eyes. They squinted as if to question, what could be so well-conceived? That's really how he pictured it.

He walked off again. Grabbed some fruit. Cherries, melon, chopped apple. A handful of everything. Plenty to go around paid for by the victims that lay about the place.

He returned and stood in front of her as she stared back blankly.

'I can't imagine a better way to… how'd you say?' and he bit deep into the handful of fruit as juices dripped instantly from his hands, 'To honeymoon… you… and me,' he smiled and looked her up and down like a farmer might a prize cow before milking.

She closed her eyes.

He grabbed her head, pinned it back. Forced her to look at him. She was clearly pained by it, he didn't care. Licked her cheek up and over an eye. Tonguing carelessly deep into the corner of her socket like he was trying to tongue her eyeball out.

He spat her salty eye fluid out.

'We will honeymoon, my sweet. We will,' he bit deep into a handful of fruit, stepped back and dripped the juice from half-eaten melon onto her face, across her mouth, then squeezed what was left across her chest and rubbed it into her breasts. Stretching his fingers between the buttons of her stretched shirt.

A giant monitor lizard walked through the food hall, stopped ten feet from Sinbad and turned slowly in judgement. A living dinosaur. Momentarily shocked by Sinbad's animalistic, primal behaviour. Now it turned back to its own hunting.

'What you want, fucker?'

It hissed, unperturbed and moved off. Legs splayed.

'Was it Billie Holiday? That song?'

She looked back at him ferociously. A wild animal— like the monitor lizard.

'That song?'

She said nothing. Her mouth wasn't gagged anymore.

'Speak bitch. Open up. You better. And... get used to opening up... I have something for you, coming very soon,' he smiled. 'I'm just waiting for the call.' He took his mobile from his pocket and put it on one of the tables by them.

Its screen was a ticking bomb. Waiting to go off.

Sinbad hadn't noticed the rest of the pirates quieten down, disappearing off into a silent place. *They must have found a young girl or boy to play with*, he thought.

He'd been so focussed on Cherry, the main course in the food hall. They could have the snacks at the side tables. He'd take all seven tight purses from her and be back for dessert.

Silence.

She smiled at him.

It was strange, he thought. *Why?*

Had she come round to accepting her fate? A last fuck maybe? He didn't like it. He wanted resistance.

He puzzled at her face.

It was like she'd gone off to another place. The wind now blew the canopy to the food hall and in a sudden gust, she sighed as if she'd breathed the wind in and out of herself. Like she was part of nature and the elements. The building. Everything all around them.

Sinbad was rattled. And that didn't come easily.

There were no lizards, no birds. The light was changing.

He sensed it. He knelt to pray.

It was too late...

He saw her smile again. Full of love. At something behind him. As two skewers came through his lungs and chest. Then came arms as if in an embrace.

'Goodnight Sweetheart...' she said. 'Happy honeymoon.'

'I only have eyes for you,' another voice came from by his ear. Then, a bloody hand outstretched and held her face in front as if it was his own.

Sinbad dropped to the floor, alone.

The monitor lizard looked at him from under a table, now it had company. It had been sleeping, now it had a mate. They looked hungry, like they wanted him. Sinbad's flesh. His tongue and eyes.

He slowly opened up his mouth so it could see inside and take him.

21

THE CHASE

THE BIG AMERICAN slurped down the noodles like a fat hog at a trough as local market traders and fellow diners, usually polite, reserved and self-contained, looked at him with an equal measure of fear and disgust as the drips, sinew and matter flew from his eager jowls.

He was like Henry the 8th feasting in celebration of a battlefield victory he'd left prematurely—so arrogant and sure of victory. Failing to get blood on his own hands.

The Fatman had glory on his mind and his stomach needed filling. It was always the case. In the past, he'd often raided the fridges of his victims and then need to take a shit. The adrenalin and food was an explosive combination. He took great pleasure in it all: blood, shit and dollars

In a few hours that would be it. The trinity complete.

'Tickity-tock, motherfuckers,' he said out loud. Imagining all that money. Both from the island and a tasty transfer of the remaining payments from his employers; those sorry fucks who'd paid him to take out John Black. He just needed Sinbad and his band of merry little fuckups to finish up over there on the resort and they'd all be on their way. And he'd rest up for good.

He wished he'd hung around. Seen the sharks tearing into John's flesh. It was a done deal. The cage had gone down with him passed out and cut up in it. What tiger shark wouldn't lap that up? Although, he half wished it wasn't done: the game. He saw now how he could get paid all over again by another load of saps to take John down again. He was an easy target to taint and take the blame. Lee Harvey Oswald times a thousand. Quite a tidy money-spinner. Easy to paint black for any occasion.

His stomach rumbled as he looked around. Unnerved by a change of wind. Seeing things, ghosts.

Shadows, shapes, anything could be John. A spectre. A shape passing by.

His stomach went again. 'You must be fucking joking. I don't have time for this,' and he stood impatiently looking around for a toilet sign before it was too late. The rumbling meant only one thing: he had to go.

He slammed the door behind him and in a splash felt two stones lighter.

He left the box room make-shift bog to return to the market stall cafe table.

'What's it with you people?' he looked down at a frail old lady with a carrier bag of bloody, nondescript meat that she was trying to sell to the noodle bar owner. He snatched the bag from her and she started screaming like a wild banshee.

He lifted his shirt, and they looked puzzled at his enormous belly.

Then, he lifted a fold of flab that covered his pistol. She calmed back down to her normal yammering level.

'Universal language, isn't it? The gun.'

'Fatty,' the chef said in the background and turned back to his cooking.

The old lady nodded quietly. Returned her focus to the rancid meat he'd snatched from her. Looking like all she had to sell to the World. Like him, probably just doing what she knew to get by. Just trading in a different sort of death.

'Now, what the fuck have I been eating here. What's in this bag?' he peered in, 'I can't tell if it's a skinned cat or a hairy lizard—what the fuck?!' he gave her the bag back and shook his head. 'Now give me a fucking Coke to wash this shitty taste outta my mouth,' he said to the man who turned back to serve him.

As the Fatman sat back down the mobile he'd left on the fold-out table lit up, started vibrating and he snatched it up as a spray of spit and Coke flew and dropped to the laminate tabletop. Another old lady shook her head and he throttled her slowly in his mind. His eyes narrowed in a threat she'd be hard to forget.

He waited, looked at the flashing screen of his mobile and took another gulp of Coke as a passing school girl cast him a glance like he was a disgusting pig.

He was.

He shot another look back at her. Scorning fire in the eyes. A return back at her like she was already dead, bleeding out of every hole as he squeezed the life from her throat with a heavy army boot. It was an easy image to conjure. He'd been there before. She looked like she could see it in him. That he had done all those things and more.

She ran off scared.

He looked at the mobile phone's screen again: *Sinbad.*

He was a bit disappointed everything was going to plan. *About fucking time,* he thought. *End game.*

'You'd better have finished cleaning up over there, Sinbad?' he answered.

He was answered with a hiss, waves. A bird. Just the island replied back.

'You gone mute? Bring the fucking loot over here and let's get it divvied up and be on our merry-fucking-way. I'm done with this sweat-box you call home. And… send me a pic of you fucking that bitch, Cherry. Play airtight with her. Every hole, Sinbad, you hear?!'

Hiss. Crackle. Hiss.

'Send them. I'm serious. I need one or two for the wank-bank! Been a while since I had anything juicy,' the Fatman didn't stop to let the person on the phone get a word in. He started to bounce a little on the bench seat with excitement. Counting dollars in his head. Seeing flesh and blood. 'And… where's the one of John Black getting ripped apart by sharks? I was looking forward to that with my lunch. You know the fucking plan, Sinbad. I need that pic, sailor boy.'

He heard crunching down the line, like an animal feasting on gristle. Then shouting. A guttural scream.

Then came a voice:

'The plan's changed. Sinbad is with a couple of horny lizards. They're finishing with his tongue. Moving on to dessert: his eyes.'

'John-fucking-Black.

A lizard's hiss came as a reply.

'Sharks must have better taste than to chow down your sorry-ass.'

A crack came down the line. Maybe a gunshot. Maybe a neck pushed hard in the wrong direction.

The Fatman was immune to fear. 'Just give up and take a bullet, will you? I get paid, and the world's a happier place with you not in it. Drop-dead, John. Easy-as-that.'

'That so, Fatman.'

He grinned as the market froze still all about him. Disposable bodies paused in their frenzy—hanging on his words and actions. The Fatman had half hoped it would come to this. He knew he'd tempted fate, had been lazy, procrastinating the *end game* over food.

Really, he knew he'd have to finish it up himself. It was always his show. And his stage to pull the curtain. Fuck it, it should have dived in the water and eaten him himself.

'You could have taken those lads out, John, in Ireland,' the big man taunted John. 'Instead, they did some easy time. Real easy. Then got out didn't they, and what did they do, John? Only went on to nail bomb a load of innocents. If there is such a fucking thing,' his hand gripped the receiver hard. 'That's on your conscience, John.

Nothing down the line—dead air.

'Now, do the decent thing, will you? Take the ticket. You deserve it for the victims' sake—drop the fuck—DEAD.'

'They were young enough. To have a chance... I gave them one,' John's voice spoke with the distortion of hate and a bad reception.

'Shit it, John.'

'The prison system had other ideas.'

'How'd you Brits say? Bollocks, pal! You just fucking bottled it. Didn't take the shot. Didn't follow orders. I should know. It was my-fucking-order JOHN!. And now...now, you've gone on to be as much a criminal as them. In Manchester. Salford. And your fucking books, don't get me started. They are criminally-shitting-bad too, John. You can't write your way out of this, Johnny Boy.'

'That so?' a whisper.

'Now you've got a lady caught in the middle too. Tasty. Real sweet, lover boy. Just do it for all of us, and die. Will you? Go on.'

'You'd do well to leave her out of it.'

'*That* so…' the Fatman copied.

'She's got a sharper bite than me.'

'On my cock, John'

Dead air.

'I'll soon see anyway, John, I'm coming back over, to pay her a little visit. You had a lucky break last time. I should have watched you get torn to pieces in that cage. Rather than drown. Oh and, John…'

The market started to reanimate. Canopies blew as if defrosting and people raced to be everywhere and nowhere at all.

'…don't worry. I'll deal with your little bitch whilst I'm there. I'll even let you watch if you're a good boy.'

John breathed hard down the line.

The big man grinned, loving the true glory of it all coming to light, 'Save me a seat at the restaurant over there on that island, John, you interrupted my dinner here. I'll finish chowing down on your bitch!'

'Don't bother.'

'What?'

'I'm already over the other side…

'Wh…?'

'…on that side, with you.'

The big American stabbed the phone screen with a chubby finger leaving a residue of chicken, noodle soup and something worse behind. He was that animal. The one the bystanders thought he was.

He stood up and walked as if drunk, swaying back and forth, into the main flow of pedestrians, down the central market lane, scanning as he went. All the faces. All the shadows.

Birds flapped under the canopy overhead. Making their escape as the people all around stopped, freezing again, then parted in front of him. A sea of betrayal to the Fatman.

He saw him, John, fifty yards ahead. Staring back. Standing still. A monument to his final project, not yet over. A masterpiece.

Stillness, again.

A dove flew from one side of the market overhead to the other; getting out of the firing line.

Like two sharks in a small tank. There was no room to manoeuvre and no sense of who was going to attack first. But they would, it was in their nature. Feral beings with razor-sharp teeth.

The Fatman stared back. Dead. Statuesque too.

John looked like an upright shadow. All in black. He'd taken one of the Pirate's outfits and his face was covered in blood. Like Martin Sheen in Apocalypse Now. Dragged through Hell leaving Hell worst off.

'I love that film,' the Fatman said to himself, smiling.

The crowds were like statues too, still, caught in time. Forming a clear line of sight. A tunnel between the two men.

'What's it gonna be, John?' the big man muttered to himself and slowly went for his gun. *I might get him from here, doubtful,* he thought and he flicked the safety off. 'So, let's bring down chaos,' he said and raised the gun anyway.

John didn't seem to flinch.

Why would he? A shadow.

The Fatman started firing indiscriminately into the crowds at the side that instantly sparked back to life. A young girl screamed, gripping her leg as blood sprayed. A boy's face gushed as his cheek exploded claret lumps onto a stall that sold once pure white sheets, and a dog yowled, then quickly silenced by the bullet that passed through its chest. Its tail stopped moving like a flag between breezes.

Screams kept erupting, echoing all around.

Stalls were toppled as people scrambled to escape the firing line in sheer panic.

Chaos. And in it, the big American was gone.

The big bang—then blackness.

JOHN SPRANG TO action and ran through the melee at the spot where the large man once stood.

Then he paused.

In the distance, he saw a moving shape, a mass, another stall toppled, and clothes and fruit flying in the air as a familiar shape bundled through. A fat bull in a china shop.

He set off again, chased hard, then stopped to refocus.

Up ahead: screams, another gunshot. Yelling. That shape again, barging. The panicking crowds parted and there it was again. That mass: the Fatman, like a fucking black bear. Heaving, growling, scowling at him. The Fatman raised his gun at John, smiled and then fired into the crowds anyway, again and again, this time where some old people were cowering. He didn't seem selective. An old lady screamed, pushed back by a bullet as an old man she was with toppled to one side as his knees shattered to oblivion.

John gritted his teeth.

This bastard was something else.

The Fatman was toying with him. Even worse he seemed to see these people as disposable assets to distract John into his grip. By shooting into them like they were deadwood. It wasn't going to end quickly. The game the Fatman played was ugly.

Again, the big American was gone—disappeared. John couldn't understand how he moved so fast and with any stealth. Or, how he sweated so little for such a large man. What he was sure of was that with the threat of death the Fatman willingly opened any door he liked. And simply could just disappear, in a flash. It was like he'd found the keystone for the bridge of his success. And pushed at it relentlessly without care for those cowering underneath.

John panted, waited for the next taunt. Then it came.

A message flashed up on the phone he'd called the Fatman on:

John,
You better hope you get to her before I do.
Goodnight sweetheart.
X

It could be a distraction. To get rid of him whilst the Fatman made his escape. John couldn't afford to take the chance. And he knew in his gut this was the way it was always going to be.

John replied back after he'd sprinted to the nearest jetty and boarded the first boat he scrambled into:

She's killed bigger than you.
I'd run in the other direction, Fatman.

23

OLD LADY ON A PLANE

THE OLD LADY on the plane to Borneo had retired translucent skin. The couple sitting next to her must have been able to see her bones through it. Her fingers moved and stretched the wet tracing paper-like membrane that held her dry brittle bones together.

Clickety-click they went as the shards of bone accentuated her words, like knitting needles threatening to split that wet-paper-like skin at any moment.

She'd listened to their own stories. Extracts anyway. Small sound bites from short lives hardly lived—mere hundred-metre dashes, she'd said flippantly. When she was nearly finished her version of life: the Olympics and was gasping her way through her part of the last marathon, sprint or relay. *Relay* being re-incarnation. Passing one energy off to another. If they believed in such things?

They nodded as if they might do, believe that is, and weren't closed-minded souls after all.

That looked like it made her smile.

She seemed to wait for her moment patiently then let them have her insights. Wisdom of the ages. Eagerly telling the newlyweds she'd never been to the places they'd mentioned: Manchester, Bristol and beyond. Not many big cities for that matter. That she might like to, maybe, one day. That was if she lived long enough—she was getting on a bit now. She made that clear. Over and over.

And she was scared of them, the cities. That was made clear too.

Who knew... when the race was run? She quipped. Smiling and giggling as if her inevitable demise was a punchline to a joke she'd already heard before. Everyone's and anyone's life, she said, is the same for that matter. A foregone conclusion.

She preached to them, by being *that* old she'd cheated death long enough. Had had her time. That it was *their* generations that should be wary. Maybe a sprint was all they had in them? And whoever looked over the sports field of life, had plans to change the track, close the games down altogether...early. Before a storm hit.

She'd made it clear she'd heard there were lots of gangs, particularly in Manchester. And that, most definitely, wasn't for her. Gunchester she'd heard Manchester called. The papers were full of it, she admitted. But also, that there wasn't smoke without fire. Or, a body with a hole in it without a gun or knife in someone's sorry hands somewhere.

The plan became a library. And their bank of seats and echo chamber.

The man of the couple adjusted himself in his seat at her words. Like she'd touched a nerve or could see into him. deep, dark and down to his roots: the books he'd written, still had in him.

It was like they were looking through her skin again. Glancing sympathetically. Down to her own core and they saw a bloody sage in her, as she was commenting on their time together.

Despite the man's slight discomfort, she went on anyway. The old lady saying that Bristol, or Brissle—however you say it—was full of rum-soaked modern-day pirates too. Wenches—drunken hen dos and horny stags. And…we all knew what they got up to. Didn't we?

She giggled and again her fingers went clickety-click.

There was crime everywhere. She made that clear too, that she understood it like her palms—In both cities. All cities. Breeding grounds for heathen chemistry. Rogues, vagabonds and strumpets.

She said she knew it had scenery, Bristol. And it had the Gorge, the Suspension Bridge, SS Great Britain…but, she'd be too scared to go out and see any of it, if she made it there at all. That the tourist traps would be lost on her completely. She might as well watch it all on the telly.

She rambled on like this for most of the journey.

She might have napped if the storm hadn't hit. Sometimes the couple gestured as if to notice her words, sometimes not. The old lady just kept going, seemingly glad of the company. Relentless.

She talked and talked.

Then, it dropped: it had happened to her cousin, apparently, *crime* that is.

Her cousin had become a lock-in. Was all a bit crazy, the old lady had said gleefully as if sharing a box of cream doughnuts.

It was a bit of a self-fulfilling prophecy that came true for the man, her story unfolded. He was a widower—just like her. Both of them, it would seem, to her, missed death only to be reminded of it every day by the absence of someone. *Such is life*, his glance at the window said.

The woman of the couple next to her shifted this time as if seeing a premonition, the woman now seemed to fear her new husband's untimely departure.

Life's irony was in the title, the old lady had said: *Life*. Because in the end, we're all going sometime. Some taken too soon and wishing not. And if they get a chance they should think on it.

Then, there were the others, she said, with days drawn-out beyond appreciation. A grey monotony. No better off, some might say.

Life.

Yes, she said, life was a curious contrary beast. In the end, biting everyone and everything.

Chomp— chomp. Her dentures clashed together through a wise old smile.

Maybe they should have gotten together, the old lady shrugged and continued: her and that cousin of hers that became a lock-in. Widowers together. Partnered by their loss. It wouldn't have worked out, she confirmed eventually after much remuneration. Answering a question the couple hadn't asked.

It wouldn't have worked, no. Not the way he was and ended up at the end of his own race—a sorry state of affairs. No chance of that...she preached. Almost convincing herself.

Clouds gathered and filled outside the cabin's shell. Only man made deep, when the words she cast transcended everything.

She didn't know what it meant anymore anyway, she'd said: to be a couple. Together. Forever. Or, at least part of the way of the journey together.

Her words unwittingly undermined the couple's place on the plane. John and Cherry didn't appear to mind. They could have moved or asked her to stop.

They didn't, and she went on.

Her story continued: the change in her cousin, the lock-in, came about when he had answered the door to a delivery driver one day, you see. Nothing happened. Just a delivery for a couple next door who weren't in at the time. They were in Costa delsol, Portugal, St Lucia…Sardinia. Somewhere like that. And somewhere neither of the old people could afford to be going themselves. Neither her, nor the lock-in.

The Borneo trip was paid for by her son, she'd said. And, that they needed to catch up. And…he wouldn't come to her. So he had paid for her to get to him. Generous in material wealth. Less so in empathy and care.

The delivery driver and parcel to her cousin was innocent, she started up again, after apologising for the random-tangent. Yes, innocent, but, when the man sat back down from answering the door, that afternoon's nap brought images and evil dreams drenched in paranoias. Visions. Illuminating everything dark that could have happened if the delivery man had been a different soul: an evil being crossing his path. Ringing his bell. Crossing his path with fear, hurt and blood.

So that was it, her cousin never left the house again, she said. A lock-in.

The man chose to trap himself inside his semi-detached bungalow, with his own thoughts and dreams—the very things that had bestowed the darkened imagery in his mind, to begin with. And to rely on deliveries himself to exist.

Such is the matrix of fate…and hate, she'd told the couple, as her aged digits stretched that thinnest of canvasses again over her hands again and again.

It wasn't an evil killer, just some poor innocent delivery person you see. Her cousin's mind had filled in blanks that just simply weren't there. A sorry state of affairs. The delivery driver could have been a saint or a killer. Not on that day though. He just left the parcel for the Auster and Cusk couple next door and then, quite politely and innocently, trudged off back to his van.

On the clock you see.

All of us time-pressured—tick-tock, dears, she said, Tick. Tock. She tapped her frail old wrist where a watch could have been.

The old lady seemed to distract herself back into positivity on the plane. She was clearly well practised at that. With a lifetime of incidents.

This time, she sat back and whispered about hen dos and horny stags again and giggled at her own naughtiness: filthy thoughts. As if letting the positivity flow back through her, an injection of hope.

I should write my own book, she thought out loud to them.

The man, John had shifted uneasily on his seat again when she was saying all this. It was like she'd read one of his own books. He hadn't said much about them but the old lady made a point of not liking the sound of them when he did.

The couple had only been permitted a few lines of introduction; key points before the old lady's desire to share her world had started to gush and flow.

They obviously let her talk, it was the start of their honeymoon and they were both still drunk on ideals.

They didn't appear to give her the full truths in their short replies, obviously holding back, when she asked about their own lives. They just appeared to fill in enough to be polite, give her the company she craved.

She grinned as though she loved being part of the start of their journey together. Their future love. That she might be always remembered as much as the baggage they took with them and the seats they sat on, maybe even more. Her world-weary wisdom soaked their seats and poured into the aisle.

She was…a joyful spectator. As she was nearing the end of her own life's journey, glimpsing others' trails through aged ground down lenses of her eyes.

They continued to keep their answers to her so very short. Admitting they were part truths in terms of places and general occupations: something generally creative and dreamt up for him. Likewise for her, even more so artistic, now she was an actual painter, they'd said…

Both used to be in service, they'd told her. And now needed to paint through the memories. A hint at harder things in life that she might not have been so unlucky to witness.

Her eyes seemed to blacken over temporarily at that. As if, who were they to know what she had or hadn't seen?

Everybody hurts, no?

She'd gone on like this, a sweet old lady. Of course.

Words with occasional toughened world hardened battle armour. Talking back at them, as the couple held each other, openly lost in an increasingly loved up glaze. The old lady rambled on and on as if knowing them intimately. And they smiled back at the right points, nodded along, just enough.

The old lady asked for a virgin mary. Copying John when he ordered his. She had winced and made a comment about it tasting a little like real blood: salty, irony and thick. And that there wasn't enough in hers—not enough blood that is.

JOHN AND CHERRY hadn't thought to interrupt the old ladies monologue.

Maybe they thought they'd soon forget her small talk as it added to their delusion. Escape. Distraction. Their own self-fulfilling prophetic wishes to be born on that plane. The act, dance and construct they'd made. To forgive, forget, to move on and to be better people.

The lady's soft sweet ambling tones were the best background hums and white noise. Accompanied by the engine's mechanical strength and roar. It was beauty and the beast.

The old lady seemed to convey all that her voice conveyed. Innocent. Wise. They let her wash over them. No sub-text. No lies. Just words flowing out of her. Like candy floss in the wind. And if they chose to catch it they could and ride her thoughts to another place.

Hypnotic release.

Into a rich sleep.

When the weather outside shifted, the old lady's mood seemed to too. Like she was only happy in the sun. And forever sad in shadow. Also, as if she was an integral part of all they were experiencing. As much as the metal shell protecting them from the storm and the stewardess with the virgin marys.

As the clouds collided, she had told them she had a son. That she hadn't seen him in a long time. That…he was a writer too. And, they'd lost touch. Would see him again when the plane landed.

Then, the lightning crashed as if threatening all she held on to in seeing her son was being questioned.

Life couldn't answer all paths, possibly taken, all the time. But, the cracks sometimes show through to another path taken—as the lightning ripped the canvas of one place to glance at another.

John and Cherry closed their eyes tighter, seeming to sleep even deeper through the storm as it built to a crescendo. Conditions that would wake and terrify anyone else. In contrast to the old lady, who now shook her words out, it was as if life's torment and chaos brought a familiar blanket of calm to the couple: John and Cherry.

THEY COULD HEAR her shaky commentary, massaging them into a deeper and deeper sleep. Better than ever. No wave machine could ever compete. They were off to dreamland in the flick of a switch.

When they woke, the whole cabin braced. As if having been forced to crash land. Everyone was on the other side of panic and fear. Recovering slowly. Some still panting. Others shaking heads in disbelief or trying to reorganise their perceptions of what had gone on.

Rips in time and place, lighting sharp.

Unfazed and untouched by whatever had held the cabin, John and Cherry smiled and checked their tickets and the glossy leaflet to their luxury resort again, for the twentieth time. A beautiful place. With images of giant monitor lizards, giant book swaps, troops of monkeys, spaces to think, swim, float and just be. Photos of hornbill birds and glorious hotel suites on stilts out into the beautiful azure ocean waters.

They couldn't wait.

The old lady looked exhausted. Her sharp mini breaths gently rocked all their seats in tiny jolts. The echo chamber was drawing to a close.

The couple closed their eyes again and imagined where they were headed—the perfect island hideaway.

What could possibly spoil it?

Some of the last words they heard her say, as they descended back into conjoined images, was when she told them: to enjoy their trip, my dears. That they should remember her cousin and estranged son. That the story is only as true as the one you tell yourself. And, that if you let the darkness in…it will, take over. She might have held their arms as they slept. They felt something. Maybe it was for them, or, her own comfort as the storm raged. To borrow their calm spirits. Unfazed whilst under fire.

She had whispered: not to let the nightmare in. That we all have to go sometime. And again: it's all about *that story* we tell ourselves in getting there. To keep that darkness out.

Then it came, before the veil of deep sleep drowned the storm, or the old lady and plane's humming droned out for good…

Her words fell like those of the barman's, from Chapman's Bar on the beach resort they would eventually arrive at:

'In the end. Are any of us really here at all?'

24

THE STORY

JOHN REMEMBERED THE old lady on the plane. Her words. Her translucent fading skin. Was this the end to the story they'd been telling themselves?

He put his arm around Cherry as they both stood in the stains of impending aftermath.

He'd won the race to the island. And in getting to her.

The finishing line wasn't there in front of them yet.

Their journey was uncertain: a marathon, sprint or relay. The old lady had spelt it out like she'd already run their race. He doubted now if there even was one: a finishing line or an endpoint. And, that all this torment was for something he'd done in a past life. Way beyond the bombers, gangs and words he'd written. Wars raged. One man or twenty.

The waves outside crashed as a warm wind attacked the palms and canvas canopies over their heads.

The birds and lizards prowled the destruction of the food hall looking for scraps and gourmet treats amongst the blood and bodies. John knew the Fatman wasn't far away, would be arriving any time soon. If he wasn't there already.

Then...he appeared.

Of course. Arrogant and swift.

With no pretence at stealth, there came a thump thump of his shoes on decking. As naturally as one of the monitor lizards passing or those hornbills landing. Brazenly strolling through the screen of bamboo plants at the front of the food hall and then pointing his gun straight between them both.

Then he focussed in on just her.

It was all about knowing what button to press.

All in one unlaboured fluid motion. Inevitability. Feeling like everything had already happened and they were reliving it in the words of a book. A replay on screen. Act upon act, a distorted VHS getting grainier with each viewing. But still, returning to have another experience of it.

They'd been here before.

This edge of death threat was familiar—but no less savage to them. John and Cherry thought they'd left the violence. Now, they realised it would never go as the big man casually aimed and squeezed the trigger enough to let them know it could all be over in a split second. Or, it would just start over—another cycle—never-ending. Like bloodletting to an ancient curse.

The waves crashing outside. Black as hell as the clouds overshadowed them. Sun up. Sundown. Cycles of inevitably, and life.

Clearly, the Fatman was delighting in the whole experience of what had transpired so far. Like the animals that had gatecrashed the restaurant. He looked as happy as a wild boar at a banquet. Feasting on the occasion with other peoples' blood at his feet.

The pressure in his chubby trigger had it all. The story they told themselves. And that it had all come to a head in this. An ox of an index finger. The epicentre of their universe rested on the pressure that thick tip exerted.

'He won't do it,' the American said, looking at John's own hand. It had raised, automatically, with a gun already in it. It was as if the Fatman had noticed before John and Cherry had; that

John's reflexes had raised the gun so naturally. A limb reflex. His instinct to protect. To kill.

The Fatman smiled like a viper.

'He won't fire. Never does it. Why do you think we're in this fucking mess?' the smirk on the American's face leered and morphed at them like the Joker, less the make-up.

The sounds of waves came from the nearby shores. Inevitability drawing near.

Black and white flashes of hornbills flew overhead under the stretched canopy as another two waddled through the mini warzone. They were retaking the island now the Pirates were dead. Also, they are oblivious, uncaring to the confrontation below. More in search of more scraps and discarded meat from the buffet that lay by some outstretched dead legs. Added together with flesh from the bodies of a dead chef and a customer wrapped together in an accidental bloody embrace on the floor. Caressing a giant spilt plate of Nasi Goreng.

It could still be their story: John and Cherry's.

Like the old lady on the plane had said. All they had to do was shift gear. To look at the sun. Keep hold of the baton until it was time to it pass on. Don't let the darkness fully in.

John already had, to get this far.

It wasn't time for the red tape. A finishing line. The baton wouldn't be passed on.

The American held up an ID Badge. Prick loved it. It was obvious to John and Cherry. And in a second they felt the abuse of power he'd wielded with it. It looked like part of his anatomy, fixed and joined to him forever. A virtual cock.

The Fatman held this tiny sheet of laminated card out. Pointed to them, a barrier.

John had Cherry. His own strength. A shield made of granite, steel and Vikings.

The Fatman went on, 'Imagine the storm you'll kick up when they find you've killed an agent. You are a hated man, John, across the U.K. already. I've made sure of it. Sponsored a city-centre bombing, pretty much,' he smiled and shrugged. 'The U.S. will jump at the chance to join them in hunting you down after. Jumping on the hate machine against you.'

John's right eye tightened down the barrel of his handgun.

'You see it's all about the story we want to believe. Isn't it, John? The one we chose to tell ourselves.'

The old lady's voice from the plane echoed in John's head: *There's not enough blood in my bloody Mary... It's all about the story we tell ourselves.'*

'You'll have nowhere else to hide, John. I found you, here. Easy. You're not hard to track. Dragging this cunt-bitch about,' he waved his gun up and down Cherry's frame. Like he was stroking it with his fingertips.

She stood strong alongside John as if they held each other up by just being there, together.

They all tensed. The birds stopped pulling an eye from a chef's socket. The lizards stopped slopping about in a blancmange.

'CUNT. BITCH. AROUND.'

The big American's words dropped like a grenade between them. Echoing off the hard marble walls. With it resonated the pinnacle of everyone's time together. Captured by the room and animals that had turned up to witness it. They all knew—destiny— fate— the universe:

Now, time was finally up.

'Shoot the fat bastard,' Cherry said.

Softly spoken words, embracing their calling. John could read her feeling every syllable.

She surely felt the same: if they couldn't run from the violence they'd chase it down. Purge every place they came to next.

They'd write their own story rather than be slaves to it.

'Shut the fuck up, bitch,' the American barked, rasping, spitting. So full of spite and venom.

The Fatman was a fat walking snake. A demon with an ID badge, waving it in front of his face like it was something they should yield to.

'I fucking hate authority,' John said finally.

The Fatman smiled back, holding the card like it was an iron shield and that it represented some higher power: bulletproof respect. Something that shaped his world. Even now. Against bullets.

It's all about that story... we tell ourselves.

'Shoot him,' she whispered. Sweet, on a gust of air. This time seductive. Whispered. kissed. Lover to lover. A touch of death.

John fired: CRACK.

The bullet passed through the ID card and into the big man's face and out the back.

CRACK. CRACK. More shots.

A spray of matter dropped, matching the pink blancmange at the Fatman's feet. Then, another rang out, a chest shot clean through and out the back. Spraying the curtains and a couple of hornbills before the big man had a chance to fall and the birds to fly off. Instead, he stood, staring. All the birds too; as if stuffed. waiting for the curtain call.

The island's waves, rain and winds beautifully masked the sounds of flesh and bone parting as the blood sprayed up the ivory white walls.

'There's the shots I owe you big man,' John said.

The room, a chamber, seemed to record every word.

'The ones you ordered me to take back in Ireland,' John stamped out the history between them.

The Fatman took a step back. Dead and dying, somehow still able. An overweight Frankenstein.

A set of plates slid then smashed in the background as a bird took flight. The china exploded into a thousand pieces. Separated by the fracture. Always brought together by their original form.

Then he toppled, the Fatman, falling like a huge giant redwood. Splintered and cut in two, bleeding out like a tap had been turned on. Flowing freely.

John walked up to the huge evil lump on the floor, fired again; another one in the head and another in the lungs, just like training... and then some more.

For them. All of them.

Then another two: bang, bang.

'And there's two more for us,' he said.

Cherry moved alongside John. Love creeping back into the room, 'This wasn't quite the *adventure together* we had planned. Was it, pet?'

'No...'

She held his arm, pulling it down from its aiming position. Holding his hand like he was a small boy just having killed a sparrow.

'...but it fits, doesn't it?' John whispered between the sounds of waves. Smiling.

'Still happily married?' Cherry asked, questioning everything that had come to pass.

'More than ever,' he smiled, then some more. He didn't look back at her, he knew she was too.

Perfect love.

'HAS THAT PLANE moved?' John said from the sun lounger next to Cherry as the host of black police boats approached.

'Which one?' she put a hand up casually sheltering her eyes from the sun, searching the sky as to where he was looking.

'That one,' he pointed, again. 'It never seems to move. It seems trapped in mid-air. And I'm not sure if going up or down. Are you?' he sat up and folded his Moleskine shut as his black pen rolled off into the sand.

He laid back and closed his eyes. To dream a new story. Or, an old one told a different way.

He imagined the plane full. That each seat was taken by an enemy, a friend, a family member and other authors. Then, he visualised it crashing down into the sea: food for the sharks. Snapping, gnawing and biting. Flesh ripped. Bones crunched and on fire.

He opened his eyes.

The police boats by the beach had switched their engines off and were hovering away from the jetty. Coasting. Like they were making a landing strategy, or just giving the waring couple a moment.

Waiting to make sure the coast was clear. No danger left.

They didn't know if the war was over yet. In fact, all that was left was a clean-up. John and Cherry had cleared and cleaned up them all.

John opened his eyes wide to see black silhouettes against a glaring sun. Then he closed his eyes tight shut again as if remaking their existence in a blink. He re-opened them again, having repainted them both with his mind.

'It's whatever story we tell ourselves,' he said to the sun.

'What are you writing this time?' Cherry asked, laying back as she picked up a bloody dog-eared copy of *The Last Llanelli Train* she'd found on the beach.

'Untethered,' he said, staring at the spot in the sky where the plane once was.

'Haven't you already written that? It was your first book.'

'Not like this,' he answered, lifting a rolled cigarette to his lips and reaching with the same hand to a bottle of dark rum that rested in the sand as if it was bounty from a shipwreck.

Cherry outstretched her own hand with a black Zippo lighter in it, flicked it open and snapped it alight. A souvenir she'd taken from the Fatman.

John drank the dark rum down, smiling all the way, and breathed in a smoke as she held the flickering flame by his face.

She was together with him in that flame.

Ahead of them both on the beach, the police boats eventually landed.

Hesitantly, characters dressed all in black walked up the beach. As they disembarked, their boats bobbed as if catching the waves of a large object that had crashed in the distant waters. A plane maybe. The same waters that had rescued John earlier. Re-birthed him. Time and time again back with a Viking inside of him.

John swallowed up his thoughts, his past fictions ripped apart like the night skies as he reopened his notebook and started over again. Re-writing history.

Dark shadows marched up the beach—an army of new ghosts to take over. The characters passed John and Cherry as if they were invisible. No threat. A dead island in their wake.

'Are any of us really here at all?' John said, repeating what the old lady had whispered to them both on the plane. When they were at the start of their journey. Before time was re-written.

But for the words, blood and violence, it was as if they were never really there. It was as if the stories they told themselves, that's what made it real: *Untethered. Transference. Division* and *Viking.*

These were the stories they told themselves.

ABOUT THE AUTHOR

John Bowie was born in Northumberland, Northern England.
He has published poetry, short stories and several novels,
including the *Black Viking Thrillers*. He studied in Salford,
Greater Manchester, in the 1990s. He now lives in Bristol, U.K.
John is the founder and editor-in-chief of Bristol Noir.

Twitter: @johnbowie
Web: www.author.johnbowie.co.uk